TEXAS Hold'Em Made Easy

A Systematic Process For Steady Winnings at No-Limit Hold'Em

WALT HAZELTON

Copyright © 2024 **Walt Hazelton Publishing**

All rights reserved. No part of this publication may be reproduced, distributed, or transmitted in any form or by any means, including photocopying, recording, or other electronic or mechanical methods, without the prior written permission of the publisher, except in the case of brief quotations embodied in critical reviews and certain other noncommercial uses permitted by copyright law. For permission requests, write to the publisher, addressed "Attention: Book Rights and Permission," at the address below.

Published in the United States of America

ISBN 978-1-963379-91-4 (SC)

Walt Hazelton Publishing
222 West 6th Street
Suite 400, San Pedro, CA, 90731
www.stellarliterary.com

Ordering Information and Rights Permission:
Quantity sales. Special discounts might be available on quantity purchases by corporations, associations, and others. For details, contact the publisher at the address above.

For Book Rights Adaptation and other Rights Permission. Call us at toll-free 1-888-945-8513 or send us an email at admin@stellarliterary.com.

About The Author

Walt Hazelton has been playing poker of one kind or another for over 60 years. Texas Hold' Em became his favorite over 20 years ago during which time he played primarily in on-line tournaments. He has a degree in Mechanical Engineering from the University of Pennsylvania and an MBA from the Wharton School. He is a retired Management Accountant from Xerox Corporation. He later joined Gunn Partners Consulting where he helped large corporations improve their accounting processes. He has published several articles including "How to Cost a Labor Settlement" and "The In Ins And Outs Of Foreign Trade". He was instrumental in the development of a formula utilized by the Carter administration's Council On Wage And Price Stability (COWPS) for calculating the cost of labor settlements during a time in which limitations were placed on these contracts.

Texas Hold'Em Made Easy

Preface

Why is this book different from all the other Hold'Em books? Because it provides a systematic and yet simple process for steady winnings. It doesn't require a player to remember a lot of statistics and tables of probabilities. Instead, it allows a player to know the value of their hole cards within just a few seconds and then be able to quickly reevaluate as the hand progresses. It utilizes a simple point count approach similar to that created by Charles Goren for the game of Bridge. Using a similar process, a player can determine the worth of their cards very quickly. This system helps players avoid getting into hands with cards that might look appealing but are high risk and can lead to the loss of a lot of chips.

I have worked with this approach for over two years with steady winnings. During that time, I actually tracked the results of over 10,000 hands to validate its power.

In addition to my basic point count strategy, this book provides unique, yet easy to understand, guidance for a shortcut in determining the probabilities of certain cards appearing in the community cards. It also includes unique guidance in playing in heads-up games. It also has a chapter which covers special techniques for playing on-line as well as several chapters on the basics of playing Hold'Em.

While playing Texas Hold'Em in on-line tournaments over the past 15 years I have been amazed at how many players have played cards that have a low probability of winning. Often these players get trapped into playing past the flop when they hit something. They then proceed to play further on the hope of winning even though they have a minimal hand. This generally leads to the loss of a lot of their chips unless they get very lucky on the subsequent cards.

As an example, one of the most common problems by many players is the weak-Ace play. It seems that some players consider an Ace with any other card a good hand. Once in, and an Ace shows up on the flop, the feeling is that this is a sure winner and justifies calling or even raising a previous bettor. Sometimes this could be a winning hand but I have seen many players lose big pots with weak-Ace hands.

Wouldn't it be helpful to such players if there was a simple way to evaluate their hole cards so that they don't get into a hand with cards that are a long shot? With that in mind I decided to develop a valuation process for Texas Hold'Em. I proceeded to create a relatively simple technique and then used it for over a year while playing in on-line tournaments. During that time, I also watched how some of the pros handled certain and decided to make a few changes to my system. I then tested this improved system by keeping track of my results while playing over 10,000 hands. I was very excited about the results which has emboldened me to write this book.

Clearly such a valuation process is only one aspect of playing Texas Hold'Em. However, getting off to the right start on each hand is critical, which is the focus of the first few chapters of this book. Many of the other aspects of playing are also covered in the later chapters so that a player can be successful in a variety of situations.

Of note is that this system is particularly well suited to no-limit tournament play. This could be a single table tournament or multiple tables. It is a conservative approach to the game that allows a player to steadily grow their chip stack the same as I have done over the past two years.

Table of Contents

1 Hold 'em Basics 1
2 By The Numbers 15
3 After The Deal 23
4 The Value of Position 28
5 After The Flop 34
6 The Rule of 48 44
7 Pocket Pairs 49
8 Connected Cards 64
9 Playing With an Ace 70
10 Reading the Board 79
11 Stack Size 87
12 Trapping 91
13 Changing Gears 97
14 Bluffing 102
15 The All-In Bet 107
16 On-line Strategies 112
17 Early Position Strategies 118
18 Momentum Plays 122
19 To Muck Or Not To Muck 127
20 Quick Thoughts 141
Glossary 143
Appendix 149

1

Chapter One

Hold 'em Basics

Even Though Texas Hold'em is a relatively new card game it has quickly become one of the most lucrative games available. It can be played live in casinos, in other local establishments or it can be played on-line. In this chapter we will cover the basic rules of the game as well as some of the more common definitions.

Types of Hold'Em Games

Before getting into the details, we need to describe the various types of Texas Hold'Em that most are commonly played:

Limit Hold'Em

Each player receives 2 cards and then 5 are placed in the middle of the table for all the players to utilize in any combination to make a hand. The amount of bet or raise any player can make is a set amount.

No limit Hold'Em

Each player receives 2 cards and then 5 are placed in the middle of the table for all the players to utilize in any combination to make a hand. Any player can bet up to all of their stack at any time.

Omaha Hi

Each player receives 4 cards and then 5 are placed in the middle of the table for all the players to use in any combination except at least 2 of the player's 4 cards must be used. Only the high hand wins.

Omaha Hi/Lo

Each player receives 4 cards and then 5 are placed in the middle of the table for all the players to use in any combination except at least 2 of the player's 4 cards must be used. There are two winning hands: a high hand and a low hand. One player could win both the high and the low by using different combinations of the cards available.

The strategies covered in this book are geared to playing no-limit Hold'Em. However, many of the evaluation techniques can apply to the other variations although not as well to Omaha where each player receives 4 cards.

The following describes the play for no-limit Hold'Em:

The Table Set-up

At the beginning of first hand in any tournament a dealer must be determined. This is done by dealing each player one card. The dealer will be the one with the high card. Where two or more players receive high cards of equal rank such as two Aces the dealer is the one with the highest-ranking suit. (Spades are highest with Hearts, Diamonds and Clubs following in that order.)

The player with the high card is the designated dealer. However, he or she will not actually deal the cards in most tournaments. Instead, there will be an official dealer who only deals the cards. In on-line play this function is handled by a computer.

The player receiving the highest-ranking card, as described above, is designated as the dealer and is given a marker (a button was used in the early days) so that it is clear as to who the designated dealer is. This position is often referred to as being "on the button". The cards are then dealt starting with the player immediately to the left of the designated dealer. This person is in the "small blind" position. The next player after the "small blind" is referred to as the "big blind". These terms will be used throughout this book.

The Blinds

When Hold'Em was first created the question was how to ensure there would be some action on each hand. It would be very boring if everyone chose to check after getting their two cards and everyone would get to see the community cards without any increase to the amount in the pot. So, instead, mandatory bets were established for the first two players after the dealer.

Before any cards are dealt the amount of the mandatory bet is specified. The player in the "small blind" position must put in chips equal to ½ of the specified amount. The player in the "big blind" position must put in the full amount of the specified amount. These amounts are referred to as the "small blind" and the "big blind". As additional hands are played the "big blind" amount will increase on a predetermined schedule.

Antes

In addition to the blind amount that is required of the first two players to the left of the dealer, all players may be also required to put in an ante. This is not always done in the early stages of a tournament. When it is required, the amount will also increase on a regular schedule as additional hands are dealt.

The Deal

Once the small blind and big blind players have put in the required amount, as well as any antes that might be required, the deal can begin. Each player is dealt two cards. These cards are called the "hole cards" and are not shown to any of the other players. The player immediately to the left of the "big blind" position (often referred to as being 'under-the-gun") is the first person to declare their intention. If their two cards are not desirable, they can fold and the hand does not cost them anything more than the ante, if an ante was required. If they want to stay in the hand, they must put in an amount at least equal to the big blind. Or, they could raise by the amount of the big blind thereby putting in twice the amount of the blind. They also could put in more than that if they choose. Each subsequent player must either fold, call the amount previously bet, or raise. Any raise must be at least equal to the amount of the previous raise. (When a player stays in the hand by only putting in the amount of the blind it is referred to as "limping in").

After all the initial betting has been completed the dealer puts aside (burns) the top card of the deck and then deals the next three cards face up in the middle of the table. (This is generally referred to as the "flop"). These three cards will be referred to as "community cards". They are used by any player that is still in the hand to augment their holding. The remaining players must then decide whether they want to make a bet or just check. The first player to the left of the dealer, who is still in the hand, must indicate whether they are going to simply check or make a bet. If this player just checks then the next player must decide whether to check or make a bet. If any player makes a bet the subsequent player(s) have three choices. They can fold, they can call by putting in the same number of chips as the previous better, or they can make a raise which has to be at least twice the amount of the previous raise.

Once this round of betting is finished, the top card of the deck is burned and the next card placed alongside the previous three in the middle of the table. (This card is often called "4th street" or "the turn"). This additional card can then be used by the remaining players to improve their hand. This means, of course, that, of the total of six cards that each player now has available, one will not be utilized to determine their best holding since only five cards are used to determine a winning hand.

Another round of betting takes place at this time, again starting with the first player to the left of the dealer that is still in the hand. A decision to check or bet is the same as described above.

After the betting is completed the top card on the deck is "burned" and a final card is placed in the middle of the table. (This card is generally called "5th street" or the "river.") At this point there are five cards in the middle of the table. Each player must determine how best to combine their two-hole cards and the five in the middle to maximize a five-card holding. (There will be times that the five community cards are the best possible hand so that the two cards that a player holds are not used.)

Once the five cards have been dealt in the middle of the table the remaining players can either check or make bets starting to the left of the dealer. Once the betting is complete the player who made the last raise must show his or her cards. Any player with a better hand must show their cards. If a player does not have a better hand, they can discard their cards without showing them if they wish. (This is referred to as "mucking"). Also, if no other players call the first better, that person will win the pot and does not have to show his/her cards.

In order to better understand these rules, we will walk through a typical hand.

Sample Hand

This hand is being played in a no-limit tournament where all the players paid $10.00 as an entry fee and were given $3,000 worth of chips. For this hand the ante is $10 (antes are not required in all tournaments) and the blinds at this point are $50/$100.

For purposes of describing how a hand is played we have set up a table with eight players and numbered them in sequence starting to the left of the dealer.

(The dealer position rotates around the table for each new hand so for the next hand the dealer would be in seat we have shown as #1):

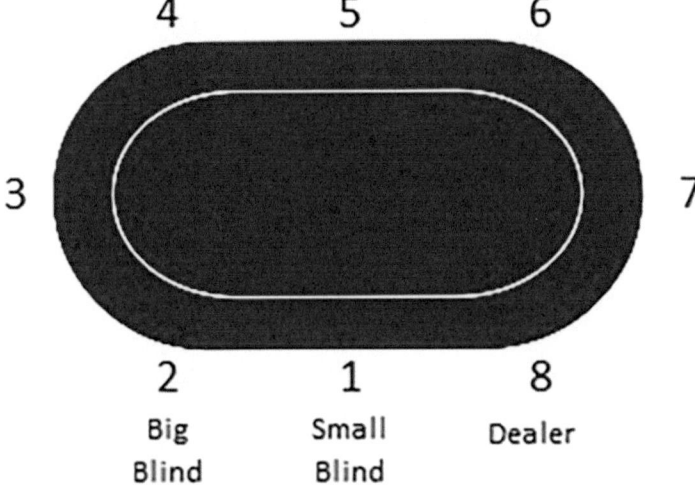

Before any cards are dealt each player must put in the $10 ante. The player in the small blind must also put in $50 worth of chips and the player in the big blind position must put in $100.

Once the antes and the blinds are put in, cards are dealt, face down, around the table starting with the player in immediately to the left of the dealer (seat #1 in our example). Once all the players have their two-hole cards the first round of betting can begin. In most traditional poker games, the player immediately to the left of the dealer would be the first one to make a bet. However, in Texas Hold'Em the player immediately to the left of the dealer (seat #1) had to put in the small blind amount ($50) before the deal and therefore has already made a bet. Also, the next player to the left (seat #2) had to put in $100 before the deal. So, these players are not the first to act after the two-hole cards have been dealt to each player.

Instead, the third player to the left of the dealer is the first to declare their intentions for the hand. (Seat #3 in our example) This is the unique feature of Texas Hold'Em which makes sure there is some betting in every hand. This player is often referred to as being "under-the-gun".

Player #3 has three choices:

1. Fold

2. Call

3. Raise

If the player folds no more chips need to be put in. If they choose to stay in the hand they can "call" by putting in $100 worth of chips. They could also announce a "raise" which would require putting in at least $200. The raise could be more than $200 if they desired. The raise could even be as much as all their chips.

For purposes of this sample hand, we will assume that player #3 folds. The action would then go to the player in seat #4 who would have the same choices. We will assume that this player "calls" by putting in $100 worth of chips.

Each of the subsequent players would have the same three choices. (Fold, call or raise.) We will assume that the player in seat #5 folds, the player in seat #6 calls and #7 folds. Player #8 also calls by putting in $100 worth of chips.

The action is now on the Small Blind player (seat #1) who had put in $50 in chips before the deal. That player now also has the same three choices as the previous players but if that player wants to just call, they only have to put in $50. If they want to make the raise, they would have to put in at least $150 to bring their total to $200. ($50 to call plus the minimum raise of $100). We will assume this player just calls by putting in $50.

The action is now with the player in the Big Blind position (#2). This player has only two choices:

1. Check

2. Raise

Since this player had to put in $100 in chips before the cards were dealt, and none of the other players made a raise, this player can stay in the hand by just checking. Or this player could make a raise by putting in at least $100 more in chips.

For this example, we will assume the Big Blind player checks so this round of betting is complete. The table would then look like this:

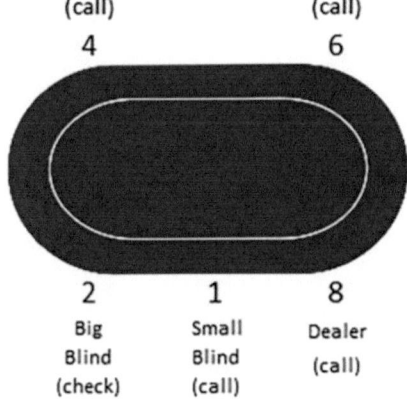

At this point the dealer discards the top card in the deck (commonly referred to as "burning) and places the next three cards, face up, in the middle of the table. (This is called the "flop".) These cards are community cards. They are used by all the remaining players to make a hand.

A new round of betting now takes place starting with the first player to the left of the dealer who is still in the hand.

In this case it is player #1 who has two choices: check or bet. If they check it goes to the next remaining player who would then have the same choices.

We will assume that players #1 and #2 both check but player #4 announces a bet of $100. This is the minimum amount that could be ventured. (This player could have bet any amount more than $100, even all of their chips.)

At this point the action moves to the next player that is still in the hand which is #6 in our example. This player has three choices: fold, call or raise. To just call would require putting in $100. We will assume this player wants to make a raise. The minimum would be an additional $100 for a total of $200 which is what this player chooses to do.

The action now moves to the next player still in the hand which is #8. The same choices are available. They could fold, or call, by putting in $200, or raise. A raise would require a minimum of $300 ($200 for the previous bet plus a $100 raise) the raise could be any amount above that as well. We will assume this player just calls.

The action would now move to the small blind player but before moving on, this is what the table would look like:

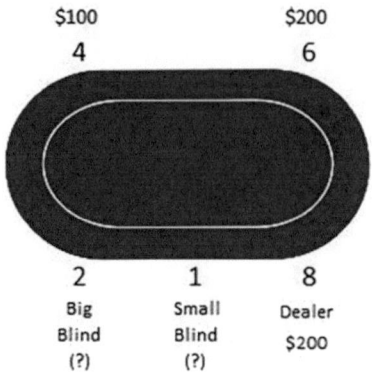

The two players in the blinds had checked when this round of betting started but now, they must decide if they want to stay in the hand which would require a minimum of $200.

We will assume the small blind folds and the big blind calls. The action now goes back to player #4 who again has three choices: fold, put $100 in to call, or make another raise. We will assume he calls which concludes this round of betting since all the players have called the raise made by #6.

The dealer now burns the top card in the deck and places a fourth card in the middle of the table. A new round of betting now starts.

The first player to act is again the first player to the left of the dealer that is still in the hand. In this case it is player #2. Here again is a unique feature of Texas Hold'Em. In most traditional poker games, the first person to act at this stage of a hand would be the last person to make a raise. (Player #6 in our example.) In Texas Hold'Em it is always the first player to the left of the dealer.

Player #2 has to decide to check or make a bet and decides to check. Player #4 has the same choice and decides to make a bet. In any new round of betting the minimum is the amount of the big blind which in this case is $100 so that is what is bet by #4. Player #6 can fold, call, or raise. Calling requires an amount of $100 and a raise would have to be at least to $200. Player #6 decides to make a raise of $150 by putting $250 into the pot.

Players #8 and #2-fold at this point because it would cost them $250 and they have to wonder what player #4 might do since that player still will have an opportunity to make another bet after they play.

Player #4 actually just calls and the dealer can now discard one more card and put a 5th card in the middle of the table. It is now up to player #4 to decide what to do: check or bet. The minimum bet is again $100 but it could be any amount above that.

We don't need to go any further with this since the rules of betting are the same as after the 4th card was added to the community cards. Once the betting is finished the player making the last raise must show their cards and the high hand wins. (It is also possible that all other players will fold so the one remaining player wins.)

To determine the winning hand the players, use any combination of their two cards and the five community cards. They might use both of their hole cards and only three of the community cards. Or, they might use only one of their hole cards and four of the community cards. In rare instances they might use all five of the community cards if their hole cards don't provide a better hand.

Ranking of Hands

For players totally new to poker the following definitions may be helpful starting with the highest possible hand.

Straight Flush

Five consecutive cards in the same suit such as a J-10-9-8-7 of Hearts. This is the best possible type of hand and can only lose to a higher straight flush. When the straight flush is A-K-Q-J-10 it is called a Royal Flush and is the highest hand possible.

Four of a Kind

Four cards of the same ranking such as 5♠-5♥-5♦-5♣. It is a rare holding but can lose to a higher four of a kind but only if there are two pairs in the community cards.

Full House

Three cards of the same rank plus two of another rank such as J-J-J and 9-9. This type of hand can only occur when there is a pair in the community cards.

Flush

Five cards of the same suit in no particular order of ranking such as A♥–J♥-9♥-7♥-6♥. When there are two players holding a flush, the winner is the player with the highest card. A flush can also occur when all five of the community cards are of the same suit. In that case the pot will be split between remaining players unless one of the players has one or more of that suit in their hole cards and then the high hole card determines the winner.

Straight

Five consecutive cards in different suits such as A♣ -2♣ -3♥ -4♠ -5♦. The winning hand is the one with the highest card. In the example including an Ace the high card is the 5.

Three of a Kind

Three cards of the same ranking such as 7-7-7. This is a strong hand even though not very high on this listing. It is often referred to as a "set".

Two Pairs

A hand with two pairs of equal ranking cards such as Q-Q and 10-10.

High Card

There will be times when no player has one of the above hands in which case the player with the highest-ranking card wins. If more than one player has a card of the same ranking the winner is determined by the ranking of the next card(s) in each hand.

Below is a chart with the order of ranking:

Straight Flush
Four of a Kind
Full House
Flush
Straight
Three of a Kind
Two Pairs
One Pair
High Card

Summary

The number of chips a player must put in to play a hand are as follows:
- Small blind: ½ of the blind amount
- Big blind: equal to the blind amount
- Calling: equal to the previous amount bet
- Raising: at least twice the previous amount bet but could be any amount higher than that

2

Chapter Two

By The Numbers

The essence of this book is to provide an easy to remember system for successfully playing hold 'em. It advocates a conservative approach to the game that will allow consistent winnings.

The Point System

The "By the Numbers" system gives points for every combination of hole cards. The number of points will dictate how a player acts in each hand. A certain number of points are required to play a hand and a greater number are required to make a raise or call a previous raise. After the flop the total points will likely change based on the community cards and this will then dictate any subsequent actions by each player.

Basic Point Values

The basic points are as follows:

$$A = 15 \text{ points}$$

$$K \text{ \& } Q = 10 \text{ points each}$$

$$J \text{ \& } 10 = 5 \text{ points each}$$

There are no points given for cards below 10s.

So, for example, hole cards of an Ace and King would be worth 25 points as would an Ace and Queen. Holdings of King and Jack would be worth 15 points.

The chart below shows all the possible values:

A A	30
A K	25
A Q	25
A J	20
A 10	20
K K	20
K Q	20
K J	15
K 10	15
Q Q	20
Q J	15
Q 10	15
J J	10
J 10	10
10 10	10

A and 2 thru 9	15
K and 2 thru 9	10
Q and 2 thru 9	10

J and 2 thru 9	5
10 and 2 thru 9	5

Pocket Pairs

Two cards of the same rank, known as pocket pairs, certainly are more valuable than two of different ranks. To recognize this, 30 additional points are given to pocket pairs regardless of the ranking of the cards. Thus, in the above table, two Aces would be given an additional 30 points thereby raising that holding to 60 points. And, while cards below 10 did not have any value by themselves, where they are a pocket pair, the hand would have a value of 30 points.

Suited Cards

Another combination that deserves additional points is two cards of the same suit regardless of ranking. For this situation an additional 10 points are awarded. For example, and A and Q of the same suit would be worth 35 points as compared to 25 points when not suited. Similarly, a 9 and 5 of the same suits would have a value of 10 points.

Connected Cards

Another combination that is given additional points is connected cards, which are two cards just one ranking apart. Thus, and A and K would be given 10 additional points as would an 8 and 7.

For instance, here is a hand I played recently:

 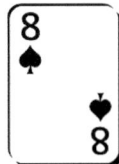

These cards had a value of 20 points. (10 for being suited and 10 for being connected.) I was in a late position and was able to limp in. Other players had folded around to the player on the button who held:

 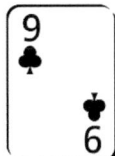

He also limped in. The small blind folded and the big blind checked. The flop was:

  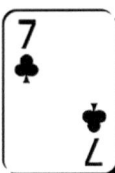

The big blind checked and with bottom pair I also checked. The person on the button with top pair bet the minimum and the big blind called. With such a small bet by the person on the button I felt my flush draw warranted staying in the hand. The turn card was the 8 of diamonds.

 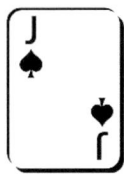 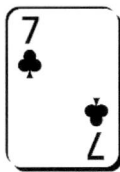 

I was now holding two pairs but they were bottom pairs so I checked again. The button raised three times the blind. Since the person on the button had only made a small bet after the flop, I figured he probably didn't have an Ace. At this point I had to look at the amount I could win compared to the amount to call. My two pair might be enough to win but I also had a draw to a full house as well as a flush. The amount in the pot was now nine times the big blind and I would only have to put in three times the big blind so I called again. The river card was the 4 of diamonds. Since the other players had not previously made any significant bets, I bet three times the blind amount and was called by both players.

In this example the power of both suited and connected cards allowed me to stay in the hand past the flop and was rewarded by winning a large pot.

Summary

While all the above illustrations of point value may seem complicated at first, it can be quickly converted to memory. It is as simple as the chart on the next page shows:

	Points
A	15
K & Q	10
J & 10	5
pocket pairs	30
Suited cards	10
Connected cards	10

The chart on the next page provides some examples of how these combinations work for a variety of hole card combinations.

	Card Values	Pair Bonus	Suited Bonus	Connect Bonus	Total
A A	30	30			60
A K suited	25		10	10	45
A K unsuited	25			10	35
A Q suited	25		10	10	45
A Q unsuited	25			10	35
A J suited	20		10		30
A J unsuited	20				20
A 10 suited	20		10		30
A 10 unsuited	20				20
A 9 suited	15		10		25
A 9 unsuited	15				15

Other Hole Combinations (applies to all cards 9 or lower)

9 8 suited	0		10	10	20
9 8 unsuited	0			10	10
9 7 suited	0		10		10
9 7 unsuited	0				0

3

Chapter Three

After The Deal

In this chapter we cover how to use the value of your hole cards in determining whether to play the hand at all, to raise, to call a prior raise, or even to re-raise before the three community cards are dealt.

<u>Minimum Requirements to Play</u>

Once the hole cards have been dealt and you have determined your hand value using the point system outlined in the previous chapter, the question is "how many points do I need to play this hand?"

The answer is simple. ***Your cards must have a value of at least 20 points to warrant further action in the hand.*** While there are a few conditions that allow playing with fewer points, the rule of 20 points is the underlying basic strategy that should be burned into the player's mind. (Some special conditions will be covered in later chapters.)

For example, and Ace with any other card 10 or higher is enough to warrant playing the hand. However, an Ace with a 9 or lower is not enough unless they are suited cards. Similarly, a King with a Ten is only 15 points and not enough to limp in when not suited.

The other bonus that might apply is the "connected card" bonus. So, while a Queen and Jack of differing suits are only 15 points by themselves the connected card bonus brings the value up to 25.

There is also the pocket pair bonus. Without this bonus a pocket pair of 9s or lower would not have enough points to warrant further play. With the 30-point bonus these hands are playable.

The chart on page 29 shows all the possible hole card combinations that have a value of 20 points or more and are therefore the hands in which a player should consider participating. Where the point value is just 20, or even 25, only a limp-in bet is justified. But, where the value is greater than 25, a raise is appropriate.

	Card Values	Pair Bonus	Suited Bonus	Connect Bonus	Total
A A	30	30			60
K K	20	30			50
Q Q	20	30			50
J J	10	30			40
10 10	10	30			40
A K suited	25		10	10	45
A K unsuited	25			10	35
A Q suited	25		10	10	45
A Q unsuited	25			10	35

Hand					
A J suited	20		10		30
A 10 suited	20		10		30
K Q suited	20		10	10	40
K Q unsuited	20			10	30
Q J suited	15		10	10	35
J 10 suited	10		10	10	30

Other Combinations (applies to all cards 9 or lower)

9 9	0	30			30

How much to Raise

The greater the number of points in the hole cards the bigger the raise should be. Thus, for hands valued at 30 or 35 points the raise should be the minimum amount. For the 40-to-50-point hands the raise should be 3 or 4 times the amount of the blind. (See more details on raising in Chapter XX.)

Calling Prior Raises

The same general guidelines apply when there is a raise by a prior player. If it was a minimum raise then you can call that raise with hands with a value of 30 to 35 points. A re-raise would be appropriate with hands of 40 points or more. However, when the prior raise is a large one the choices become more limited. The safe play is to call with hands of 40 or 45 points but re-raise with 50 points or more. As will be described in later chapters, there are a number of additional factors that might impact one's strategy when other players have raised but in these first few chapters the intent was to keep the strategy as simple as possible. Once this has been mastered the additional strategies can be used to further improve the number of hands that are won.

Playing in the Big Blind and Small Blind positions

The point system applies the same for playing in the blinds prior to the flop. The big blind position has already put in the amount required to "limp-in" so when no other player has made a raise this player has a free ride to see the flop regardless of the value of his/her cards. However, if another player has made a raise the guidelines apply the same as any other position at the table, namely that the cards must have a value of more than 25 to call a raise.

The small blind position is somewhat different in that he/she has put in ½ of the blind amount. If no other player has made a raise only the other half of the blind amount would be required to continue play. In this case only half the points that would otherwise be required to continue are needed. Thus, with only 10 points in a hand this position could limp in. When a prior player has already made a raise, the basic guidelines would apply.

Summary

- A minimum of 20 points is needed to play a hand
- A small raise can be made with 30 or 35 points
- A large raise can be made with 40 or more points
- A re-raise can be made with 50 points or more

4

Chapter Four

The Value of Position

The position of a player with respect to the dealer has value all by itself. The reason is that after the flop the person on the button gets to see what all the others players are doing before making his/her play. In cases where the flop is neutral and the other players have checked, a raise in the dealer position will often "buy" the hand.

Playing When on The Button

As pointed out above, the person who is on the button is in a powerful position. Therefore, this position deserves an additional 20 points. This means that if the other players have only limped in, the person on the button should get involved in the hand even with meaningless cards. A limp in, or even a raise in this position, can be justified on the possibility of buying the hand. Even after the flop there can be a bluffing opportunity where other players have checked or made minimum bets.

The reason this position is so powerful is that after the flop you are the last person to play. You get to see what the other players are doing before making your decision.

For example, you are on the button and hold:

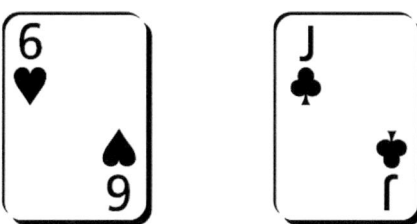

Two players have limped in ahead of you. Even though these cards are only worth 5 points this is an ideal place to go ahead and limp in. If there is no raise from the blinds then you get to see the flop with the minimum outlay. (If no one ahead of you has even limped in you might want to make the minimum raise to test whether the players in the blinds are intimidated enough to fold thus allowing you to buy the blinds.)

For instance, once the three initial community cards are dealt you can then react based on what the other players do. If all the remaining players check after the flop, then a bet from you will often buy the pot even with meaningless cards such as above. However, when there is a raise by one of the other players after the flop you will need to fold unless the flop significantly helped your hand.

Sometimes the flop will produce interesting cards such as a pair:

This presents several opportunities. First, when there is a small bet ahead of you, a raise will make the other players think you have a set of 3s or that you might even have limped in with a pocket pair of Queens.

Another possibility would be a flop such as:

In this case a raise by you would suggest you caught a flush.

However, as will be described in a later chapter on bluffing strategies, you must not always react the same way in these situations or else the other players will catch on and take these hands away from you.

Here is another example of how easy it is to use the button position to pick up some chips. This is an example of a hand I recently played. I was on the button with:

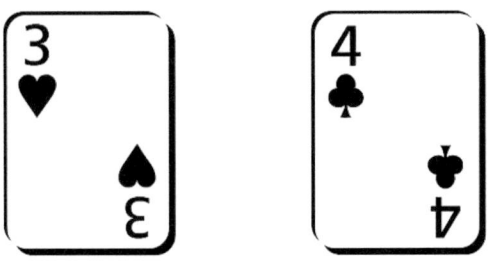

Two players ahead of me had limped in so I did also. The big blind checked. I therefore got to see the flop shown below with a minimal outlay:

 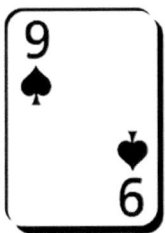 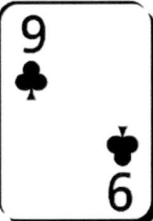

All the other players checked around to me so I bet twice the big blind amount and everyone folded. While not a big pot it was helpful to pick it up with low value cards.

Playing In Early Positions

The opposite situation applies when playing in an early position. When there are 6 or more players at the table the early positions can be problematic. (The early positions are the first two players after the big blind.) These are the first players to decide what to do with their hands with the uncertainty of what the subsequent players might do. Thus, limping in with marginal hands (20 to 25 points) can become a bigger problem when a following player makes a raise.

The guideline for early positions is to subtract 10 points from your value. This means that holdings like an unsuited A-J or lower should not be pursued in an early position.

More discussion of playing strategies when in an early position are covered in a later chapter.

Summary

- In early positions subtract 10 points from your hand value before the flop

- On-the button adds 20 points before the flop

- After the flop the first player that is still in the hand should subtract 10 points

5

Chapter Five

After The Flop

The play after the flop is the most critical point in the hand. It is the point at which players must re-evaluate their situation. In this chapter we look at a variety of possibilities and a number of charts are provided at the end to help understand some of the impacts.

However, before getting in the specific adjustments that need to be made you need to realize how important it is to analyze the cards in the flop as they almost always will change your chances of winning the hand. Specifically, if you came into the hand with only 20 or 25 points and the flop did not improve your situation you do not want to commit more chips on the hope that a weak hand can win. (Of course, you can stay in the hand if all the other players check.) But, when the flop does connect with your hole cards in some way, you will want to become more aggressive. A number of possibilities are outlined later in this chapter.

Before getting into these such details we need to look at some general rules. For instance, there are a number of ways the flop can improve your situation:

1. The flop has one or more cards of the same value as any of your hole cards

2. The flop has one or more cards of the same suit as any of your hole cards

3. The flop has cards that connect with your hole cards such as the possibility of catching a straight

These are pretty obvious and the specific points to add to your holding are covered in detail later in this chapter.

At the same time the cards in the flop can hurt you chances because they didn't help you but may provide other player(s) with a good hand.

There are three flops that I call the "fearsome flops":

1. Any pair included in the flop when you don't have at least one of that pair. The higher the pair the more worrisome.

2. The flop has three cards of one suit when you don't have at least one high card of that suit.

3. Three connected cards in the flop when they are not connected to your own cards and especially if they are high cards.

When any of these flops occur, it is critical that you carefully re-evaluate your situation. You must think about what the other players did before the flop to get a sense of how strong their hole cards might be. If a player raised before the flop and then raises after one of these flops, you must consider folding if the flop didn't improve your hand. You might even need to give up a high pocket pair. In such a situation the temptation is to continue the hand on the hope of improving but this can lead to committing a lot of chips with a high risk of losing the hand.

The next few pages describe specific adjustments you should make to your hand valuation with the different kinds of flops mentioned above.

No Pairs or Suited Cards on The Flop

- If one of the flopped cards matches your pocket pair double your points. (An Ace on the flop when holding pocket Aces makes the hand value 100 since the original value of the pocket Aces was 50.)

- If one of the flopped cards matches one of your hole cards add the value of that card. (If an Ace add 15, K or Q add 10, etc.) If the matched card is 9 or lower add 5.

- If two of the flopped cards are the same suit as your suited cards add 10.

- If two of the flopped cards give you an open-ended straight draw add 10.

The Flop Includes a Pair

- If you hold a card the same as the flopped pair add 30 points.

- If you hold the other two cards of the same level (e.g., you now hold 4 of a kind) there is no need to add any points since this will

- be a winner 99% of the time and should be played accordingly.

- If you do not hold a card of the same level as the flopped pair subtract 10 points.

The Flop Includes Three Suited Cards

- If you hold two cards of the same suit add 30 points. (You now have a flush and depending on your high card it can be a very strong hand.)

- If you hold one card of the same suit add 10 points unless your card is an A then add 20.

- If you don't hold any of the same suit subtract 20 points. (For instance, you hole cards are A's, which were originally worth 60 points, but now you must subtract 30 which reduces your value to 30 points. This is enough to continue but only when no other player makes a raise.)

The Flop Includes Two Suited Cards

- If you hold two cards of the same suit add 20.

- If you do not hold at least two of the same suits subtract 10.

The above adjustments are depicted at the end of this chapter.

Betting After the Flop

After making the above adjustments to the value of your hand the new value will dictate your action(s).

In early positions you are vulnerable to the actions of the following players so it takes a stronger hand to continue. A good break point is 40 points. Below this just check but fold if there is already a raise. Above this be more aggressive.

In middle positions you can continue play with fewer points but you are still somewhat vulnerable. A good break point is 30 points. Below this check or fold if there is already a raise. Above 30 be more aggressive.

In late position you are able to see all the prior bets before making any decisions and therefore are able to continue with fewer points. If no raises before you, make a small raise with any holding and a large raise with as low as 40 points. There is a good chance you will "buy" the hand at this point. If there is a small raise before you, call with 40 points and re-raise with 50 or more.

Betting On 4th Street And 5th Street

As additional community cards are introduced the possible combinations of situations become huge. However, there are a few basic ground rules that apply.

If the additional cards do not improve your holding continue betting as outlined in the "After the Flop" section above.

If one of the additional cards matches a pocket pair you should increase your points as outlined earlier in this chapter. However, downward adjustments may be appropriate when the additional cards might provide an opponent with a strong hand as described below.

If the additional cards give you a flush the value of your hand increases according to the ranking of your hole card in the flush. If it is an Ace then it is likely to be a winning hand and you can make large bets. Since it is unlikely that someone has a full house, you can win large pots with this holding. (Note that a full house is only possible where there is at least a pair in the community cards.) If your hole card is not an Ace you are at risk of someone else having a higher flush and must play cautiously.

The following charts capture the adjustments described above.

One of the Community Cards Matches a Hole Card

	Original Total	Adjustment	Adjusted Total
A A	50	double	100
K K	40	double	80
Q Q	40	double	80
J J	30	double	60
10 10	30	double	60
A K suited	45	add 15 if an A on the flop or 10 if a K	60/55
A K unsuited	35	add 15 if an A on the flop or 10 if a K	50/45
A Q suited	35	add 15 if an A on the flop or 10 if a Q	50/45
A Q unsuited	25	add 15 if an A on the flop or 10 if a Q	40/35
A J suited	30	add 15 if an A on the flop or 5 if a J	45/35
A 10 suited	30	add 15 if an A on the flop or 5 if a J	45/35
K Q suited	40	add 10 if an K or Q on the flop	50

K Q unsuited	30	add 10 if an K or Q on the flop	40
Q J suited	35	add 10 if an Q on the flop or 5 if a J	45
J 10 suited	30	add 5 if an J or 10 on the flop	35

Other Hole Suited/Connected Combinations (applies to all cards 9 or lower)

9 8 suited	20	add 5 if a card 9 or lower is matched	25

One of the Community Cards the Same Suit as Hole Suited Cards

	Original Total	Adjustment	Adjusted Total
A K suited	45	add 10	55
A Q suited	35	add 10	45
A J suited	30	add 10	40
A 10 suited	30	add 10	40
K Q suited	40	add 10	50
Q J suited	35	add 10	45
J 10 suited	30	add 10	40

Other Hole Suited/Connected Combinations (applies to all cards 9 or lower)

9 8 suited	20	add 10	30

Flop Incudes a Pair

	Adjustment
One hole card same as flopped pair	add 30
No hole cards same as flopped pair	subtract 10

Flop Includes Three Suited Cards

	Adjustment
Two-hole cards same suit as flop	add 30
Two-hole cards same suit as flop and now holding top flush	add 50
One hole card same suit as flop	add 10
One hole card same suit as flop and hole cards include an Ace	add 20
No hole cards same suit as flop	subtract 10

Flop Includes Two Suited Cards

	Adjustment
Two hole cards same suit as flop	add 30
One hole card same suit as flop	subtract 10
No hole cards same suit as flop	subtract 10

While these adjustments seem complicated, they should largely be intuitive. However, when playing on-line these could be printed and kept available until the essence of them is internalized.

Summary

- After the flop the value of the holding must be revised based on the cards in the flop

- The changes that are needed should be intuitive rather than a memorization of the adjustments outlined in this chapter

6

Chapter Six

The Rule of 48

At different points in the game, it is important that a player be able to assess the likelihood of improving his/her hand. This is generally a matter of determining the probability of certain cards appearing on 4th or 5th street. To make this relatively easy I have created the rule of 48.

<u>The Rule of 48</u>

After the flop each player can see five cards: their two-hole cards and the three community cards. This means there are 47 cards left from which the 4th and 5th street cards will be drawn. The question is "what is the likelihood that a card, or cards, that I need to make a good hand will show up on 4th street or even 5th street or the odds that another player might hold a card or cards that go well with the flopped cards?"

For example, your cards are:

Since these cards are suited and connected you may limp in to see the flop:

  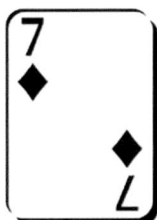

In this case either a Six or a Jack will make a straight for you. Since there are 4 Sixes and 4 Jacks left unseen, you need to figure the probabilities of either one of them showing up on 4th street or even on 5th street. So, of the 47 cards that are remaining in the deck there are 8 that will complete your straight. So, what is the probability of one of them coming out on 4th street? Doing this arithmetic in one's head is difficult. Thus, the rule of 48. The likelihood of one of 8 cards showing up next out of 48 is easy to figure out. (48 divided by 8 is 6). Using 48 as the number of cards available makes such calculations much easier than 47 and the difference in probabilities is insignificant. (The real probability would be 5.875 to one instead of 6). Even for 5th street the rule of 48 can be used since at that point dividing into the 46 cards available is just as difficult as it was before 4th street. (8 into 46 is 5.75).

In the above case with a 6 to 1 chance of getting your straight on 4th street you need to compare that to the amount you would have to bet to justify those odds and the amount you could win. If any prior bets have been small those odds might be justified. In some cases, you might want to plan to go to 5th street as well where you have two chances to catch the needed card. In that case the odds are halved and become 3 to 1 instead.

This technique is useful for a number of hand possibilities such as flush draws, two pair draws to a full house, filling a set, etc. as shown on the next page.

Rule of 48

	Number of cards available	4th street odds	4th & 5th combined
Filling an open-ended straight	8	6 to 1	3 to 1
Filling a gut-shot straight	4	12 to 1	6 to 1
Filling a 4-card flush	9*	5 to 1	2.5 to 1
Filling a set with a hole pair	2	24 to 1	12 to 1
Making a full house with two pairs	4	12 to 1	6 to 1

* With an odd number of cards possibilities, we use a nearby number to divide into such as 45

Using 48 To Assess Others Players Chances

The same rule applies to determining the chances after the flop of other players having a better hand than yours.

For example, the flop is 6-6-2. What are the chances that another player has a six to make a set of 6s? Here again, the math is very easy when using the rule of 48 since there are 2 other 6s. So, the odds of any one card being a 6 is 24 to 1. But since that player has two cards that could be a 6 the odds of either one of his cards being a 6 is 12 to 1 (two chances). If there are two other players then there are 4-hole cards that could be a 6 and the odds are halved again to 6 to 1.

These are pretty long odds and therefore would permit you to continue in the hand using the point count rules described in the earlier chapters unless there is a big bet ahead of you. If there is a small bet ahead of you, you might continue with a strong hand of your own to see what happens on 4th street.

On the other hand, where such a flop appears and you are the first bettor and you don't have a card matching the pair on the board, a raise might lead the others players into thinking you did catch a set. (More on bluffing in a later chapter.)

Summary

- To determine the probability of any specific card being dealt as the next card divide the number of such cards into 48 and then divide by the number of cards to be dealt.

7

Chapter Seven

Pocket Pairs

In earlier chapters we touched on a few strategies when holding pocket pairs but in this chapter, we will cover this topic in more detail. As described in earlier chapters pocket pairs are worth at least 30 points regardless of the ranking of the pair. This alone allows a player to play such a hand unless there is a significant raise ahead of them. However even with such a raise holdings of high pocket pairs can be pursued. The table below recaps the point values for all pocket pairs.

	Card Values	Pair Bonus	Total
A A	30	30	60
K K	20	30	50
Q Q	20	30	50
J J	10	30	40
10 10	10	30	40

9 9		30	30
8 8		30	30
7 7		30	30
6 6		30	30
5 5		30	30
4 4		30	30
3 3		30	30
2 2		30	30

Keeping in mind that it takes only 20 points to take part in a hand and with 30 or more a raise is justified. Thus, any pocket pair has a high enough value to make a raise before the flop. Since you will only get a pocket pair about every 16 hands it is important to have a sound strategy when these opportunities show up.

There are a number of considerations to keep in mind in determining your strategy for playing with a pocket pair:

- Position at the table
- The size of your stack
- The size of the blinds
- The aggressiveness of the other players
- Prior bets

These situations are often inter-related so we will look at a variety of situations and describe some alternate strategies.

Pocket Aces (60 points)

The supreme holding. One that players are always hoping for. Unfortunately, the frequency that this will occur is only about every 200+ hands. Thus, if you were to play for 8 hours in a tournament with an average time between hands of only 3 minutes, you might catch pocket Aces only twice all day. For instance, in the 10,000 hands that I kept a log on, I had pocket Aces only 38 times.

The message is that with the low likelihood of receiving pocket Aces you must strive to achieve maximum value when you are lucky enough to get them.

Before the Flop

In an early position making a big bet is likely to drive out all the other players so that all you might win would be the blinds. Instead, making a small bet is a preferred strategy. One exception to this rule would be in the very late stages of a tournament where the blinds are huge and you want to grab those chips by chasing the other players out. Another exception would be when your chip stack is very low. If you make a big bet other players with decent cards may assume you are bluffing in this situation and call your bet.

In a middle position, with no bet by a previous player, the same logic would apply. Where other players have limped in or made a small raise you might want to make a small re-raise. With a previous big raise, you would want to re-raise, or even go all-in.

In late position a larger raise is in order. Typically, this would be 3 to 4 times as large as the big blind amount. This may not drive out all the players especially any who have entered with a moderate holding. Experienced players may also assume that with a late position raise you could be trying to steal the pot. You would not want to make an even larger bet since it would likely drive out all the players and all you win would be the amount already bet. When a previous player has made a raise, you would re-raise a moderate bet but go all-in against a large raise the same as for playing from a middle position.

After the Flop

Even with pocket Aces there is a lot to consider after the flop. In Chapter Five we described how holdings are impacted by different types of cards on the flop. The best scenario would be that the flop contained another Ace to give you a set. In that case you could continue to slow-play the hand to try and extract more chips from the other players and do this by making a small bet or by just calling a previous raise. Or, depending upon the amount already in the pot and/or your stack size, you might want to go with a big raise. You can even hope that another player has the other Ace and is feeling pretty good about his/her chances.

However, if the flop was all of one suit, and not the suit of one of your Aces, a warning flag must be raised even if one of those cards was an Ace giving you a set. In an early position you should make a small bet and watch what any other players do. If they just call your bet, they are probably on a draw to fill a flush. If they make a small raise, you can call and see what happens on 4th street and even 5th street. If another player makes a large raise you have to consider giving up the hand.

When the flop includes three consecutive cards such as Q, J, 10 or even 7, 6, 5 you must be careful since there are a lot of cards that can make a straight. You should handle this situation the same as where the cards are all of one suit which is to be cautious. What other players do in this situation is extremely important. Keep in mind for them to be in the hand at all at this point means they had at least a moderate holding before the flop.

Another possible problem flop is one in which includes a pair. (Of course, if an Ace is included with that pair, you will have a full house.) So, with a pair on the flop, without an Ace, some caution must be taken. If the pair is 10s or above more caution is needed since any other players still in the hand are more likely to have a high card and could have caught a set. As with the situation with three of a suit showing up on the flop, a small bet in early position might be wise and watch to see what other players might do. Strong play by another player might indicate he/she has caught a set. You can call a small bet and see what develops on 4th street. Another Ace on 4th street would be great except the odds of that happening are roughly 23.5 to 1 (two Aces out of 47 unseen cards) so don't expect that to happen. With no bets ahead of you a raise would be appropriate but beware of a player who might check raise with a stronger hand.

Here is an example where a pocket pair shows up on the flop. You are holding:

Sitting in an early position you choose to make a small bet which is called by the player on the button. The big blind has already put in that amount and checks.

The flop is:

The big blind is now the person to act first and if he/she were to check you would want to make a continuation bet and then watch what the person on the button does. If that person were to make a small bet you would call to see what 4th street might do for you. If that person, or the big blind, were to make a large bet you should fold. (If the large bet came from a player with a short-stack and you had a sizable stack you need to make a decision as to whether this player might be bluffing in which case you can call.)

Another option in response to a small bet by the big blind, or the button, would be a small raise to test their strength.

If you were in a late position, such as on the button, and several players have limped in ahead of you before the flop, a small raise would be a good strategy in order to build the pot. Many players are likely to call a small raise since they are already invested in the hand. However, when the flop is then dealt and it includes a pair, caution must be observed as described above.

Another concern in this type of situation is the possibility that another player has a pocket pair the same as the other card on the flop in which case they have caught a Full House. In the above case they were holding pocket 10s. The only way to beat such a hand would be if another Ace showed up on 4th street. The odds of that are approximately 24 to 1 so you must be very careful to not risk a lot of chips in cases where another player is making large bets.

Finally, when the flop is neutral, such as three random cards, a small bet is appropriate in order to build the pot and drive out those who have totally missed catching anything. A big bet would only drive out all the players leaving you with only the blinds and the small bets ahead of you.

(In some of the other Texas Hold'Em books I have read several pages are devoted to how to play after the flop with pocket Aces including a lot of examples. You would have to have a much better memory than me to remember all those possibilities.)

Pocket Kings (50points)

This is obviously a very strong holding but also one that you will get only every 200 or so hands. You therefore want to maximize what you can win with it. The strategy here is almost identical to holding pocket Aces: slow play in early position before the flop and somewhat stronger play in a late position.

After the flop the play should also be similar to that described for pocket Aces except where an Ace is included on the flop. In that situation you have to be wary that another player might have an Ace which puts your hand at risk. (Keep in mind that at a table of nine players there is about an 80% chance that one of them will have an Ace in their hole cards.)

With an Ace on the flop in an early position a somewhat larger bet is in order. Any player who raises back will be telling you that he/she probably has an Ace. You could call a small raise but fold to a large raise. In late position with no bets ahead of you a continuation bet is appropriate.

And, as mentioned for pocket Aces, a flop of three of one suit, three consecutive cards, or a pair must be regarded with some caution.

Pocket Queens (50 points)

This is another of the strongest hands you will ever get and must be played to maximize your winnings. A lot of the strategy for pocket Aces applies to this type of holding as well. The difference, of course, is that there are now two cards that could show up on the flop that would raise a caution flag. When an Ace or King is included in the flop you must pay attention to what the other players do to ascertain the likelihood of someone now holding a larger pair than your Queens.

Here again, a small bet in early position before the flop is in order and a larger bet in late position. If a previous player has made a small bet a raise is in order but only a small raise. This will test how strong the other player is.

After the flop, with neither an Ace or King showing, you want to continue to build the pot with a small bet or re-raise of a prior player. Of course, pay attention to flops that are all of one suit, three consecutive cards, or a pair.

Keep building the pot on 4th and 5th streets but become increasing wary as any players keep calling especially after 5th street. If another player comes in strong at that point you must evaluate the board to see what the other player may be holding that would beat your Queens.

Here is an example of a hand played in a recent tournament:

Player in early position holds:

This player bet three times the big blind and was called by two other players. The flop is:

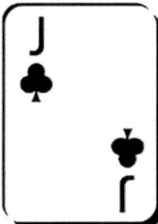 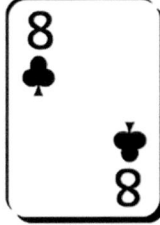 

Again, the player with the Queens bet three times the big blind. He does not want another player with two Clubs to try for a flush but a bigger bet is risky since there are two other players who may have caught something. One of the other players in this particular hand then folded but the person on the button called. The 4th street card was:

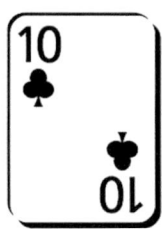

At this point the player with the Queens had to be concerned since there were three Clubs on the board. He again bet three times the big blind and the player on the button made a large re-raise.

Should the player with the Queens fold at this point? If you were in this situation you have to take a moment to imagine what this player might be holding that allowed him to call all the bets. He/she could of course have caught a flush but this is less likely because of the size of the previous bets that were called. He/she could also be holding pocket Jacks or 10's and be setting a trap by just calling the previous bets. Or maybe a Jack and a 10 and caught two pairs.

In this hand, the player with the pocket Queens didn't like the number of possibilities and folded. (The other player actually had a Jack and a 10). It takes a lot of courage to fold a high pair when there isn't a higher card on the board but one must look at the prior betting and consider what the possibilities are with the cards on the board.

Pocket Jacks or 10's (40 points)

Pocket Jacks or Tens are another strong hand that must be handled aggressively. However, it is a hand that can quickly become a liability after the flop when a larger card is included in the flop and another player makes a bet. For that reason, I like to make a large bet before the flop especially in an early position. I want to drive out players with mediocre hands that might call a small bet. Also, I don't want the big blind to be able to see the flop without putting more chips in.

In a late position, with no prior bets, a large bet is also in order. If there is a prior small bet, a raise is a good strategy and then watch what the other player does. In most cases he/she will just call your raise since your action suggested that you have a strong hand. If there is a large bet before your turn then a call is in order.

After the flop the situation can change dramatically. You are hoping for three smaller cards that are not connected or three of different suits. When that happens, you should make a big bet to try to win the pot before 4th street is dealt. If players had paid to see you bet before the flop, they must be holding something of value such as a couple high cards so you don't want to let them see 4th street cheaply. This also applies to any players that might be on a flush or straight draw.

Of course, there is also the possibility that another player has a low pocket pair and one of the cards on the flop gave them a set. This is a low probability since pocket pairs only happen about 6% of the time. A player that does get a set on the flop will undoubtedly make a large bet so you have to be cautious when a large bet is made even when the flop includes only small cards.

And caution must also be observed when the flop is all of one suit or three consecutive cards.

When the flop includes at least one high card your pocket Jacks or Tens can be at risk and this will happen often. There are twelve cards that could show up on the flop that are higher than Jack the odds of one of them being included in the flop are 1 in 4. But there are three cards in the flop so that brings the odds down to almost even. You must have a clear strategy to deal with this eventuality so we will look at this more closely.

You hold the following:

 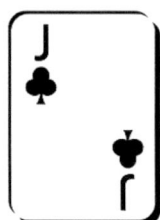

You made a bet of three times the big blind and were called by two players. Clearly, they have quality cards themselves.

The flop was:

  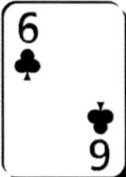

In an early position you would want to make a continuation bet to see what the other players do. If you are just called you need to be careful after the flop since the other player(s) clearly have something. If you are re-raised you might have to give up the hand.

In a late position with a relatively small bet ahead of you a re-raise will let you know how strong the other player is. Likely he/she will just call. If they raise you back then you will have to fold. Where there is a strong bet ahead of you, a fold is in order.

Keep in mind that going to 4th street on the hope of catching one of the two remaining Jacks is only practical when you can do it with a minimal number of chips since the odds of filling a set on 4th street are 24 to 1 (using my 48-point system).

<u>Small Pocket Pairs – 9 and lower (30 points)</u>

Low pocket pairs are valuable but must be handling with some caution. They carry a value of 30 points which justifies a raise before the flop. With such a raise you hope to drive out other players who hold moderate cards. You don't want to let players see the flop cheaply.

After the flop it is very likely another player will hold a higher pair since if they called your raise before the flop, they must have had something of value to begin with. And, the lower your pair the more likely another player has caught at least a higher pair after the flop.

So, before the flop, a raise of 2 or 3 times the big blind is in order especially in an early position. In a late position, when a previous player has made a small bet, a raise will put that player on the defense and allow you to be more aggressive after the flop. If a previous player makes a large bet before the flop, you should give the hand up since you will probably need to catch a set on the flop in order to continue and the odds of doing so are about 7 to 1.

The cards on the flop must dictate your play. You are hoping to catch a set which will generally be a winning hand so you will want to build the pot. If you had made the original bet before the flop and are the first better after the flop then a continuation bet would be appropriate. If there is a large bet after the flop by another player it suggests that player may have improved his/her hand. You should test this by raising back. If that player then calls your raise, you are probably still holding the best hand and can proceed accordingly. If you are re-raised your hand may be in jeopardy and you have to evaluate the prior betting and consider what the other player may be holding. Keep in mind that you cannot beat a straight or flush unless you catch a full house on 4th or 5th street. This is where the pot odds come into play. How much is it going to cost you to continue versus how much you might win?

If you don't catch a set with the flop, you are very much at risk in the hand. Here again, in an early position, a continuation bet would be appropriate. When there is strong betting by other player(s) you may have to give up the hand.

I actually prefer pocket 2s, 3s, 4s or 5s to pocket 6s, 7s, 8s, or 9s. The reason is that a lot players like to play hands with an Ace. When the flop has an Ace and a couple small cards and I am holding a low pocket pair there is an opportunity to catch a low straight. Calling a small bet after the flop in this situation can be justified when only one other card is needed for you to make such a straight. While the odds of doing so are long, calling a small bet can lead to a very large pot when the straight is filled.

Summary

- Add 30 points to your card holding value for pocket pairs

- Since only 20 points are generally required to play a hand, pocket pairs would qualify in almost any situation

With 30 points even a low pocket pair is enough to may a raise before the flop

8

Chapter Eight

Connected Cards

As describe in Chapter Two, connected cards are those that are just one level apart such as a 10 and 9. Since such a combination has more potential than cards not connected, I have given these hands an additional 10 points. This can allow some holdings to warrant playing that otherwise would not have enough value. An example would by a J and 10 which would only have a value of 10 points without the connected bonus on 10. With that added the hand is worth 20 points which allows it to be played.

When the connected cards are also of the same suit there is the added 10-point bonus. In this case even an 8 and 7 is worth 20 points. This would allow a player to play such a hand as long as there are no raises to call. Even when in one of the blinds a small raise could be called.

Also, when you are on the button with unsuited connected cards the hand can be played due to the 20-point bonus for being on the button.

The beauty of playing low connected cards is the potential of winning a big pot when the cards on the flop are helpful. The other players generally are not expecting trouble when the flop has low cards.

Of course, when your connected cards are high cards the value of the hand is that much higher and can be played aggressively as described in other chapters. But low connected cards have a unique potential so we will examine such hands in more detail here. For this purpose, we will define low connected cards are those from 9 on down.

So, in an early position with low unsuited connected cards I would fold since the value is only 10 points and there is the uncertainty of a subsequent raise.

However, when the cards are suited the value is 20 points allowing the hand to be played with a minimum bet. A small raise by another player could be called but when there is a large raise a fold is appropriate.

In a late position a small raise can be called but, without that, you could make a small raise yourself. It could be helpful to indicate some strength so that after the flop other players may check to you which could yield a free 4th street.

<u>Since low connected cards are only a drawing hand you don't want to commit a lot of chips before the flop.</u>

As an example, here is a hand I recently played. I was on the button with:

 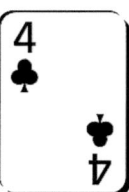

The player under the gun was holding:

And the big blind had the following:

The player under the gun made a minimum raise so I called as did the big blind. The flop was:

At this point I have an open-ended straight draw which is a long shot to fill since there are only 8 cards that would help. If either of the other players were to make a large bet I would have to fold. However, the big blind came in with just a minimum bet which the other player just called. This allowed me to see 4th street with only a small commitment of chips. The 4th street card was:

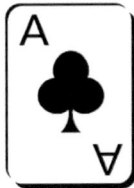

I have now filled my straight. The big blind checked and the other player, who is now holding two pairs, made a large bet. Since there is not even a flush draw to worry about, I just called and the big blind folded. The 5th street card was:

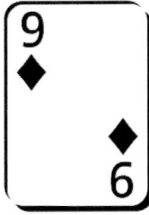

I am now holding an unbeatable hand but the player with two pairs was feeling pretty good since he hasn't been raised. He made a big bet which I raised. He called and I won a very big pot.

Suited With A Gap

After I first developed the point count system, I was not only testing it in live play but also watching the how the top pros play in relation to my system. I started to notice that a number of them liked to get involved in hands in which they had suited cards with a small gap. They were having some success with cards like a suited 9 and 7.

Clearly, they thought the potential of winning a big pot with such hands was worth a small opening bet.

Based on these observations I now recommend adding 5 points to hands with a small gap. Thus, a suited 9 and 7 would be worth 15 points instead of just the 10 for being suited. Generally, 15 points is not enough to get involved in a hand but in a late position, on the button, or in the small blind, such hands could be entertained as long as it requires only a minimum bet.

In my point count system, a holding of an Ace and Queen has a value of only 25 points in which calling a raise is not justified. However, when 5 points are added for the small gap, it raises the value to 30 where a small raise can be called. This is covered in more detail in the following chapter on playing hands with an Ace.

Similarly, in my basic point count system a holding such as an unsuited King and Jack is only worth 15 points, which is basically not enough to get involved in a hand. However, when 5 points are added for the small gap, it brings the total to 20 and the hand can be pursued.

Summary

- Add 10 points for connected cards
- Add 5 points for cards with a small gap
- Do not commit a lot of chips before the flop with small connected cards

9

Chapter Nine

Playing With an Ace

This chapters deals with hands containing an Ace, except a hand with pocket Aces which is covered in Chapter 7. In my point count system, an Ace is awarded 15 points and is certainly a good card to have but is generally not enough by itself to warrant getting involved in a hand. So, in this chapter we look at when to play hands with just one Ace.

<u>A-K</u>

A hand with an Ace and a King is a powerful hand even when not suited and therefore needs to be played aggressively. When not suited it has a value of 35 points. (15 for the Ace, 10 for the King and 10 for being connected). This means it is a raising hand.

So, before the flop, in an early position, a bet of two or three times the big blind is appropriate so that any players with moderate cards can be chased away. This type of hand will seldom win by itself so you don't want to compete against a lot of other players. If your bet is raised a re-raise is also appropriate. You are going to need help on the flop but the odds of doing so are pretty good since there are nine cards that can give you a pair as well as the long shot of a straight. You could even consider going all-in depending on the stage of the tournament, the size of your stack, and how aggressive the other player(s) have been.

After the flop the situation changes dramatically. If you catch a pair, you probably have a winning hand without further help. (Unless the flop also has a pair, three of a suit, or three consecutive cards in which case you have to pay attention to what the other players do.) So, where you have such a high pair you have some choices. In this early position it would be appropriate to make a continuation bet however if the other payer(s) have merely called your previous bet you could check on the flop and try to trap any other players. (Traps are covered in another chapter.)

When you are in a late position and have caught a pair on the flop you have the advantage of seeing what any other players do ahead of you. If they just check they probably didn't improve so you would want to build the pot with a small bet. If another player has made a small bet a raise is appropriate. Facing a large bet, you could even go all-in since at that point the only hand that you could lose to is a set or a pair of Aces when your pair is Kings. Even then you might also have a straight draw if another of the flopped cards is a Queen, Jack or 10.

When you do not end up with at least a pair after the flop you are only in a bluffing situation. In an early position a continuation bet is a good strategy. If it is just called, it probably means the cards on the flop did not help any of the other players and you get to see 4th street without committing any more chips. When 4th street doesn't improve your hand, you will want to back off to avoid losing more chips.

When in a late position, and the flop didn't help you, what the other players do is important. If they just check you can proceed with a bluff. If they make a small bet, you can call on the hope of catching something on 4th street. However, if there is a large bet ahead of you, folding the hand is sensible.

The above discussion applies when you're A-K is not suited. When it is suited it is worth another 10 points for a total of 45. This is one of the strongest hands you will get so aggressive play before the flop is warranted in any position. Since the situation can change dramatically after the flop you will want to build the pot beforehand keeping in mind that you not only have a good chance of catching a pair but also a straight or flush. If your bet before the flop is raised, a re-raise is certainly appropriate even an all-in raise.

After the flop the situation must be re-evaluated. Even when you do not catch an Ace or King you may have a straight or flush draw. These could be pursued when there is only a small bet to call. If there are large bets and the cards on the flop completely miss you a fold is recommended.

<u>A-Q</u>

A holding of A-Q is similar to the A-K described above in a lot of ways. However, it has a few less points (30 points: 15 for the Ace, 10 for the Queen and 5 for the small gap.) so a bit more caution is warranted. With 30 points, a small raise can be made before the flop, or a previous small bet called. Here also the flop will make a big difference in how to play the hand. This is strictly a drawing hand since, by itself, it would win very few pots.

This is one of my least favorite hands and several of the top pros have also indicted that this is not high on their lists. Here is a good example of how this can yield a big loss in a hand I recently played.

I was holding the following in a middle position:

 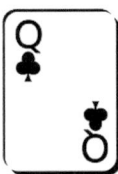

A previous player made a small raise before the flop which I called. The flop was:

 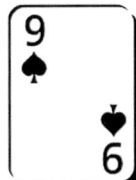 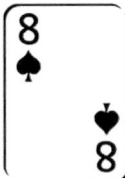

I now hold a pair of Aces with a good kicker and the previous player comes in with a small bet.

Should I call or even raise? I decided to raise back and he called so it seemed that he had a marginal holding. The 4th street card was:

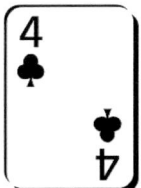

This card did not improve my hand but also didn't provide the other player with a flush or straight. That player now comes in with a large raise. He had raised early and had called my re-raise so what is he holding? There are a number of possibilities that I could lose too such as A-K, two pairs, or even a set of 9s, 8s, or even 4s. Since this player had been playing a tight game up to then I decided to fold. It turns out he was holding A-K and I would have lost a lot of chips.

A-J or A-10

An unsuited A-J or A-10 is valued at only 20 points. It is another drawing hand that has to be helped on the flop to be pursued. Limping in before the flop can be justified in the hope for some help. Where those cards are suited the value increases to 30 points in which case a raise before the flop is appropriate.

Weak Ace

A weak-Ace hand is an Ace with a 9 or lower card. Since an Ace is a powerful card, my system gives it a value of 15 points. But when the other card is a 9 or lower the total value of the hand remains at 15. (A suited weak-ace is another matter which is covered later in this chapter.) In normal play 15 points are not enough points to play the hand. As a result, there are only a few situations in which I would play a weak-Ace hand:

- In the dealer position (Any two cards can be played when there is no raise from a prior player)
- With a short stack (fewer than 5 big blinds)
- In the big blind position with no raises (a free hand)
- In the small blind with minimal prior bets

So, we will assume that one of these conditions exists and you have the following cards:

 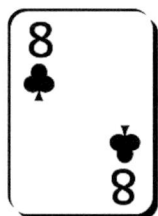

Prior to the flop two other players have limped in as well as you. The flop is:

  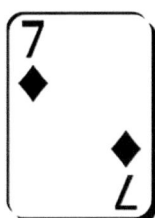

You now hold a pair of Aces with a poor kicker and no flush or straight draw. In an early position you can make a small bet to see what others might do. If you are raised, what do you do? There is a good chance another player has an A and likely a better kicker. So, if another player makes a big raise you would need to give up the hand. Even calling a small raise can be problematic especially if the card on 4th street was an 8 giving you two pair. You still don't have a sure thing especially if another player comes out strong. That player might have an A-J or might have caught a set. If you continue to play and 5th street doesn't improve your hand (which is unlikely since there are only 4 cards that could help) you might have to expend more chips just to find out you are beaten.

In a late position and another player makes a large bet after the flop, a fold is appropriate. But if it is a small bet, what do you do then? Call? Raise? Calling is tempting but then what do you do if 4th street doesn't help or is an 8 as described above? Your two pairs can be beaten in a number of ways.

With no other bets ahead of you a raise would probably get you a free card. But you are still not on solid ground if you don't improve.

The uncertain aspect of playing with the weak-ace is why I seldom will play that kind of hand.

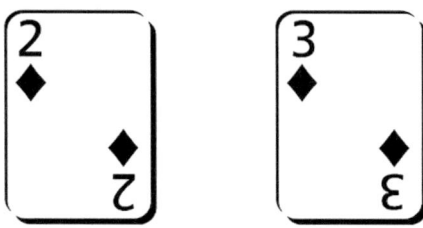

However, there is one weak-ace situation that warrants mention. Assuming you are on the button with:

You were able to limp in and the flop is:

You now have on open ended straight where any one of 8 cards would give you a very strong hand. However, the odds of catching one of them on 4th street are about 6 to 1. You could continue in this case only if it required a small bet or was checked around to you.

Suited Ace Play

A weak-ace that is suited has more value because of the added 10 points for being suited. Even then it is only worth 25 points which is only a limp-in holding. If a previous player comes in with a small bet a call can be justified to see if the flop is helpful. Keep in mind that the flop would have to include at least two of your suits for the hand to be helped and that will only happen about 10% of the time. Calling a large bet is not wise since making a flush on 4th street is another long shot (7 to 1).

Of course, filling a flush on the flop would be ideal but the odds of that happening are over 200 to 1. If it were to happen you would want to slow-play the hand in the hope that another player catches something so that you can call him/her bets and win a big pot.

Although this chapter deals with the weak-Ace play, a suited King/small or Queen/small is worth 20 points and could be played if only a minimum bet is required. If the flop contains two of the same suits further play is warranted with an added caution if an over-card is included on the flop.

Summary:

- Only play a weak-ace hand in a late position and only when you can get in cheaply

- Fold after the flop even when an Ace is included if there have been any large bets

- Limp in with a suited weak-ace to see if the flop

10

Chapter Ten

Reading the Board

In the earlier chapters we talked about how to value your hole cards. Once the flop occurs this value may change. A few examples were provided in the earlier chapter. In this chapter we go into more detail on what the cards in the flop can do to your holdings.

The Flop Includes A Pair

When two cards of the flop are paired you have to be wary of the possibility that other player(s) might have three of a kind (a set) or even a full house. If you are involved in such a hand, you must watch the betting by anyone else to get a sense of their strength. Depending on your own hand and the size of any bets ahead of you, it may be wise to fold. On the other hand, with promising cards of your own, calling a reasonable bet can be justified.

For instance, you hold the following:

And the flop is:

The original value of your hole cards was 30 (15 for the Ace, 5 for the Jack and 10 for being suited). With a pair on the board, you must reduce your value by 10 but you would also add 20 points for the flush draw. This would increase your total to 40 points. Even if you were to catch a flush on 4th or 5th street the pair on the board could allow another player to have a better hand so you have to be concerned if another player makes a large bet.

<u>Early position strategy with a pair on the flop:</u>

In early position with a value of 30 or more but no improvement on the flop you should make a small bet just to test the water. If another player raises you back a fold might be in order depending on the size of the raise. When you have a good draw, such as in the above example, a call of a small re-raise can be justified. Without a good draw a fold is appropriate. When there is a large raise a fold is also appropriate.

<u>Late position strategy with a pair on the flop:</u>

If you are in a late position with no bets ahead of you and no improvement on the flop the same strategy of making a raise to test the water would apply. If there is a small bet before you, a call can be justified even without a good draw with the chance of catching something on 4th street, or being able to buy the hand with a bluff when the original raiser checks after 4th street. With a large bet ahead of you a fold is justified the same as when in an early position.

The point here is that you must play very carefully when a pair shows up on the flop.

(Clearly when the pair on the board is the same as one of your cards the value of your hands goes up substantially. How much depends on the ranking of the cards but also would depend on the rank of your other card. Where your other card is low a more cautious approach might be in order since another player might also have the same set with a higher kicker.)

The Flop has Three Of One Suit

While a flop containing all three cards of the same suit is rare when it happens special care must be taken:

- Early position strategy

In an early position and no similar cards, it would be prudent to check and wait to see the action behind you. With any bets behind you a fold would be in order unless you have a strong hand such as a high pair. In that case a call is warranted if there has only been a small bet since you have a draw of catching a full house on 4th or 5th street. If there is a large bet a fold is appropriate. If it is the person on the button and this person has shown a tendency for strong plays in that position, and there are no other players involved, a call can be ventured.

If one of your hole cards is the same suit you may want to stay in the hand depending on the ranking of that hole card. With an Ace of the same suit you will want to make a bet early to test the water. If there are re-raises behind you just call. Keep in mind that there are only nine additional cards of that suit available so the odds of one of them showing up on 4th street are roughly 5 to 1. In other words, you would have to expect to win 5 times the bet amount to justify playing further. On the other hand, if your chip stack is relatively low you may want to go all-in since the odds of catching one of that suit on either 4th street or 5th street are only 2.5 to 1 and doubling up might get you back into the game.

If one of your cards is the same suit, but not an Ace, you may wish to continue in the hand by checking but only if your card is a high one such as a King or Queen. You can also call if a small bet has been made behind you. With lower cards it is unwise to continue unless you have some other draw such as a pair. Even then you would only continue if you only have to call a small bet.

-   Late position strategy

In a late position you have the advantage of watching the other players before making a decision. With an Ace of the same suit you can call anything but a very large bet. Without prior bets you should go ahead with a bet of your own. A large bet in this position might buy the pot but you might want to make a small bet instead on the hope of catching your flush on later cards.

With anything but an Ace of the same suit and a large bet ahead of you a fold is appropriate. With no bets ahead of you, a large bet might buy the pot. With a relatively high card of the same suit, such as a King or Queen, a call of a small bet is in order.

The Flop Includes Suited Connectors

Suited and connected cards on the flop introduce a lot of possibilities for both you and the other players. It is therefore important to evaluate what the possibilities are before even considering your own possibilities. If the cards are high ones there is likely to be other player(s) with similar high cards since they must have had something of value to have put in enough chips to see the flop in the first place. If the cards are middle range such as an 8 and 7 it is less likely any other player will have improved. With low cards, such as a 3 and 4, there is actually a somewhat higher risk since many players like to enter hands with cards that include an A and a small card. This could become a straight with further help on 4th or 5th street.

If you have not connected with a flop including suited connectors you should fold to any other bets since there are too many ways other players could improve.

If you have a small connection to these cards, such as a pairing one of your cards, you can continue to play given there are no large bets to call.

On the other hand, if you now have a draw to a straight, or a flush, you can afford to play somewhat more aggressively depending on the type of draw that you have.

For instance, a draw to an Ace high flush would be worth a bigger involvement keeping in mind it is a draw with odds of only 1 in 5 of improving on 4th street. (9 cards of the same suit out of the 47 available). A draw to any lower flush can be pursued only if there are no large bets to be called. If the draw is to both a flush and a straight then further action is appropriate if the bets are not large.

A draw to a straight is also of interest keeping in mind that another player may be playing a draw to a flush. The draw to a straight is more promising if your cards include the upper end of the straight.

For example, you are in the big blind with the following cards and there were no raises before the flop:

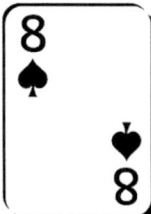 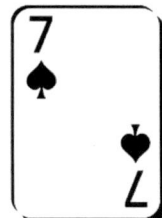

And the flop is:

 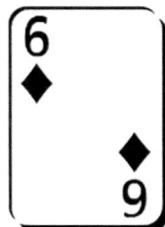 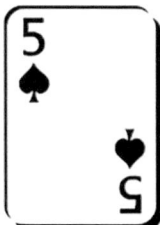

In this situation you can made a high straight with a 9 or a low straight with a 4 which would likely win the hand if no flush were made by another player.

If, on the other hand, the flop was:

  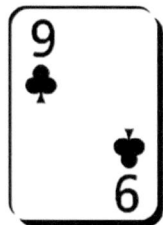

In this case your draw would be to the low end of the straight and more caution is in order since other players might well hold cards at the higher end of a straight.

The Flop Includes Three Parts of a Straight

When there are three parts of a straight in the flop you need to have some part of it to continue unless you caught at least a pair with one of the community cards and there are no large bets to be called.

If the three community cards are 10 or above there is a high probability that other players may have caught something since, they would likely have had high cards to be in the hand to begin with. In that case, if you have not improved your holdings by connecting with any of the cards on the flop and your hand is valued at 30 or less, a fold is warranted. Please refer to Chapter 4 as to how to re-value your hand after the flop.

A Rainbow Flop

A flop that contains cards of three different suits is referred to as a rainbow flop. Such flops will make the possibility of a flush by any player extremely unlikely, including yourself. Thus, even when holding suited cards, you should not continue in the hand if that is why you paid to see the flop in the first place.

Summary

- Adjust the value of your hand when the flop contains cards that can yield strong hands by the other players such as a pair, three of a suit, three to a straight or even several high cards

11

Chapter Eleven

Stack Size

At the start of a tournament everyone has the same number of chips. As play continues stacks will go up and down. This has to be considered in determining your play so we will look at a number of situations.

You Hold A Big Stack

When things are going well and your stack has grown you can afford to take some risks. For instance, you can play hands with less than 20 points in late positions. You can also make a raise in early position with mediocre cards just to reduce the number of other players.

Another situation is when you have a big stack and a short stack goes all-in. Is it worth calling just to take a chance to take the other player out? This is clearly a judgement call based on a number of questions:

- Is the all-in bet so small as to be less than 5% of your stack?
- How aggressively has the other player been up to now?
- Are there other large stacks behind you that might also call, or even raise?

You might want to make such a call with a relatively low point count in your hand if it is also a good drawing hand such as suited and/or connected cards. However, you would not want to call if by doubling-up the other player it would then give him/her enough chips to be a significant factor in subsequent hands.

Big stacks can also be used effectively with re-raises or check-raises even when on a draw. If you had made a raise before the flop players who had come in with marginal hands will often check after the flop and you get to see 4th street without a big commitment. You also have set the stage for a bluff even when the flop misses you but has intimidating cards such as a pair, three of a suit, or even a couple high cards.

You Hold A Small Stack

Sometimes you just are not getting cards and your stack is dwindling, if only through the blinds and antes. At what point must you change your approach?

At the beginning of a tournament, you will likely have enough chips to cover 100 or more big blinds. As your stack declines there is a point at which you will have to get involved even with cards with lower value. My rule of thumb is that with chips for only 10 or fewer big blinds I will want to see flops with less than the regular 20 points. This could be an unsuited weak-Ace (15 points) or a suited J or 10 with a small card, or even two connected cards. In these cases, limping in would be the strategy. With raises ahead of me I would fold and hope for better cards in the next few hands.

When your stack is down to 5 big blinds you are at a critical point and must do something dramatic. If the value of your hole cards is as low as 20 points and no one has made a raise ahead of you, you should go all-in. If there is a raise ahead of you, you must have a strong hand to call such as 30 to 40 points. When you are under-the-gun the all-in bet can also be used with hands worth only 20 points. Keep in mind that you will only get hands of 20 or more points about 25% of the time so you must play these aggressively with a short stack. Also, keep in mind that hands of 30 or more points only happen about 10% of the time so when you go all-in with only 20 points there is a low probability that another player will have good enough cards to call you.

Even some card combinations can be played with smaller values when your stack is only enough for 5 big blinds. Suited cards are especially interesting even when they are small. Connected cards are playable as well. Of course, with any cards with a value of 30 or more in early position the all-in bet should be utilized.

With a stack of only 10 to 20 big blinds bluffing is a very risky situation. At this point you have enough chips to wait for a better opportunity.

Summary

- You can be more aggressive with a large stack such as raises or re-raises even with marginal cards

- Do not buff with only 20 to 30 blinds left in your stack

- With 10 of fewer big blinds limping in with less than 20 points is justified

- With fewer than 5 big blinds an all-in bet is appropriate even with 15 to 20 points

12

Chapter Twelve

Trapping

Trapping can lead to some very big pots if done carefully. So, what is a trap? A trap is a situation in which you have an outstanding hand after the flop but you don't act aggressively. Instead, you let other players make bets and just call. This sends a message that you either have a weak hand or are on a draw. When there are no threatening cards on 4th street or 5th street you wait until your last opportunity to make a big bet on the hope that other player(s) have something of value or they think you are bluffing and call your bet.

Here is an example of a hand played in the 2013 WSOP.

Position under the gun holds:

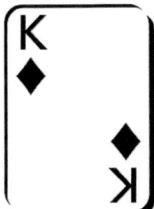 

and bets twice the big blind. Others fold to the button who calls with:

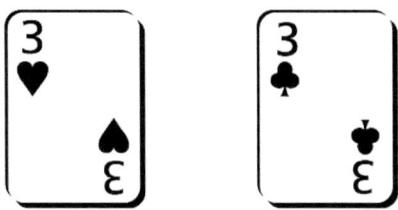

The flop was:

The person under the gun makes the minimum bet which has the appearance of only a continuation bet. This is called by the button who likes his chances with the pocket pair especially since he only has to call a small bet. After 4th street is dealt the board is:

The player under the gun now has an unbeatable full house but checks so as to appear weak. The button also checks. A three comes on 5th street so the board is:

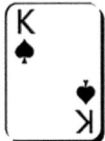  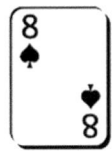  

The person under the gun now makes a bet of about half the pot which is not a large bet so the player on the button, who has caught a full house, makes a further raise. At this point the person under the gun could go all in but doesn't want to chase the other player out of the hand. Instead, he raises twice the amount of the previous bet and is called.

In this hand the player with the strong hand made three bets that all made it look like he was relatively weak and thereby enticed the other player to continue thus generating a big pot. If he had made a large bet after the flop with his three Kings, the other player would have folded and only a small pot would have been won.

However, there will be times when trying to trap that thing will go bad. It is essential after the flop to evaluate what the possibilities are for other players. This is especially true when there is more than one other player in the hand.

Here is an example of a hand going bad that I watched recently:

The player under the gun has:

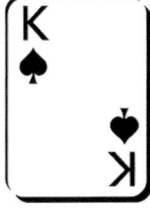 

That player decides to try for a big pot and limps in with the minimum bet. The next player has:

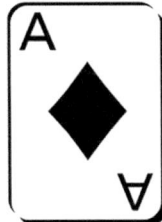 

He also decides to try for a big pot and just limps in. The player on the button has:

 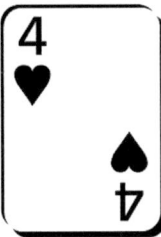

Being on the button makes this an easy call so a limping in is justified. The flop is:

 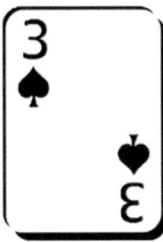 

The player under the gun with pocket Ks senses minimal risk bets three times the big blind. The player with pocket Aces decides to go for it and bets all-in. The player on the button has caught a set of 3s and calls. So does the player with pocket Kings. The 4th and 5th street cards do not help anyone and the player on the button wins a huge pot.

There were three problems with the play on this hand. First, the two players with pocket pairs made it too easy for other players to continue by just limping in. Even though they wanted to try a trap they should have made at least a small raise. Second, after the flop, they also ignored the pair on the board which should have raised a warning flag. Third, they jumped in with big bets right after the flop. Instead, they should have made small raises to see if this flop helped anyone else.

Summary

- Trapping can produce huge pots but players must be careful as the hand develops to evaluate how the community cards might be used by other players

- When the flop contains threatening cards do not let any other players get to 4th street cheaply

13

Chapter Thirteen

Changing Gears

So far in this book a very cautious approach has been described. This should allow a player to steadily increase their stack. However, to follow this method all the time can lead to predictability of what you might be holding. This is especially true in the latter stages of a tournament.

If you have rigorously followed the strategy outlined in the early chapters some of the other players will notice that you don't play hands without strong cards and that you don't stay in past the flop without a pretty good shot at winning the pot. This is fine when the blinds and antes are small. But, in the later stages of a tournament a higher risk can be justified even when it might only be to win the blinds. And, where the other players have seen you play a tight game, an occasional raise even without good cards, will make the other players think you have a very strong hand.

Here are a few simple rules on when and how to change your betting gears:

Before the flop:

- If you have been limping in make a raise when on the button even with weak cards

- If you have been playing very cautiously under-the-gun do a raise every now and then even with hands of 20 points or less

- During the late stages of the tournament big raises may throw the other players off even when you hold low value cards

After the flop:

- A raise in early position will often buy the hand even when you have not improved since a raise in this position is a generally deemed to indicate a strong hand

- A check-raise is also a very strong play especially if the previous better has not made a large bet

- In a late position a re-raise can be intimidating to the other players

If you are nearing the end of the tournament and are in heads-up play, use the 1-2-3 strategy even with low value cards.

This strategy goes like this:

    1 - fold one

    2 - call one

    3 – raise one

Not always in that order but a good mix of all three approaches. This way your opponent will have no idea of how strong your hand might be.

In heads-up you will get very few hands with big values so you cannot just wait for playable cards. It is unlikely you will get hole cards with a value of at least 20 points more than 1 out of 5 hands. So, you must be aggressive even with only 20-point hands.

Here are a couple examples of how to change gears:

- Under the gun with just 20 points make a raise instead of folding or limping in

- Under the gun with 30 plus points limp in instead of raising

- On the button limp in with 40 plus points

- After the flop and in early position made a small raise even if your hand didn't improve

- After the flop when your hand did improve just check

Another aspect of changing gears is the amount of your bets. While the above examples cover the timing of bets and/or raises, the amount you bet under certain circumstances can be varied. For instance, the normal raise before the flop is three to four times the big blind. It is good to do this most of the time but every now and then, with high point hands, change the amount to just twice the big blind. Also, with medium hands a raise of five times the big blind can be used.

And, another technique for changing gears is to modify your speed of play. In early stages of a tournament, you could play quickly when it is your turn but later on when the pots get bigger and you hold a medium value hand, a long pause could make players think you have a good hand. They might then check and you get a free card.

Another example would be to generally limp in very quickly, especially when on the button, but then later in the tournament pause for a few seconds before playing.

These are just a couple examples. There are a lot of other timing questions that can be utilized to throw off your opponents as to what you have.

Summary

- Occasionally change your style of betting, the amount of your bets, and your speed of play so the other players cannot predict your strength or lack of it.

14

Chapter Fourteen

Bluffing

In Texas Hold'Em bluffing is an essential part of the game so you need to understand how to use this strategy. Basically, a bluff is making a bet when your cards are not likely to win if other players stay in the hand. You are hoping that such a bet will drive out any other players.

A certain number pots in Texas Hold 'um can be won by only playing the hands with a high probability of winning such as has been described in the earlier chapters. However, the percentage of hands that this is possible is relatively low. In my 10,000 hands I was able to win only 13% of the time and that included some bluffs. So, without these bluffs the winning percentage would have been even lower. Therefore, to win steadily at Texas Hold'Em you must utilize bluffing some of the time.

There are several types of bluffs:

- A raise before the flop with poor cards

- A raise after the flop when your hand didn't improve

- A big raise after 4th or 5th street when other players look weak

- A re-raise with poor cards
- A raise when on a draw

We will look at situations where each of these might be appropriate.

A raise before the flop with poor cards

A raise before the flop tends to send a strong message but must be used very sparingly in an early position due to the uncertainty of what the subsequent players might do. Even then, when your chip stack is low this could be a good play as long as you have, at least, a drawing hand. When such a raise is called you will be on dangerous ground but you may still want to make another bet after the flop to continue the ruse that you have a good hand and hope this drives out any other players. You have to pay particular attention to the cards in the flop to assess the potential of those cards improving someone else's hand. If you are called, you will need to be careful about committing more chips to see 5th street. If you are raised at any point a fold would be in order.

In a late position, a raise might be sufficient to win the hand outright since there will only be a few players yet to play. Such a raise is likely to drive out the players in the small or big blind positions that do not have strong cards. This raise must be at least three times the big blind so that the person in the big blind does not get to see the flop cheaply. If your raise is called you must evaluate the cards on the flop to assess risk. If they are rags a continuation bet is in order especially when the players ahead of you have checked. If there are cards that have some value then caution must be observed.

A raise after the flop when your hand didn't improve

When you have entered a hand where the bets have been relatively low and your hand was not improved on the flop, a strong bet may win the hand anyway, especially in an early position, if you had raised before the flop. This is commonly called a "continuation bet". You, of course, with any bluff, have to pay attention to what the others players are doing. If they are just calling, they probably don't have a made hand so a continuation bet might work. If you have been raised you may want to just throw in your cards.

In a late position there are a number of situations where a bluff can work. **I find this to be one of the most successful bluffing strategies.** For instance, when a pair shows up on the flop and the other players have checked, a bet of any size will often win the pot. Also, when other threatening cards, such as three of a suit, or an Ace, or two other high cards are included on the flop and the other players check, a strong bet is likely to win the pot. I particularly like to do this when on the button and have limped in with rags.

A big raise after 4th or 5th street when other players look weak

A big raise, or even just a big bet in an early position after 4th street or even 5th street can also win pots but should be used very sparingly since the odds are higher than another player might have made a good hand by then.

Such a bet could only be justified when the other players have not made any raises or you are convinced that they are buffing as well.

This type of bluff is very dangerous as you can lose a lot of chips in the process when you are not successful. However, it is not always bad to be caught in a bluff since, later, when you made the same type of bets with good cards, you are more likely to get called.

A re-raise with poor cards

Before the flop in a late position a re-raise sends a strong message. It, of course, depends on the size of the original bet as you don't want to commit too many chips in such a bluff. But, when such a re-raise is just called you are then likely to be in control of the hand. The other player will likely be cautious after the flop unless he/she has improved. In that case a further bet by you may win the pot. I especially like to do this if I have a drawing hand so that if I am called again there is a chance of making a decent hand.

A raise when on a draw

When you have a good drawing hand a raise will build the pot and sometimes allow you to win even when you don't connect with the flop. This is often referred to as a semi-bluff. Clearly if you do connect the pot will be that much larger but if you don't a further bluff may work.

When Not To Bluff

There are a number of situations where bluffing might not be wise:

- Bluffing into a much bigger stack.

- In low stakes games there are likely to be players willing to make calls with mediocre cards

- When there are several other players still in the hand

- When an Ace or two high cards show up on the flop and any other players make a bet ahead of you

Another caution is to not do a lot of bluffing because you are more likely to get called when the other players notice that you bluff often.

Summary

- Bluffing is an essential part of the game and must be utilized in order to win enough pots to steadily increase your chips

- You must watch for likely situations in which someone else is bluffing

- It is not necessarily bad to be found out when you try a bluff

15

Chapter Fifteen

The All-In Bet

The All-In bet is a unique aspect of tournament play. This is where a player makes a bet of all of their chips. If called, it means they are either going to win a big pot or be out of the tournament. It therefore must be used sparingly.

There are only a few situations that you might utilize the all-in bet:

<u>You have less than five big blinds left</u>

When you only have five big blinds left you are in trouble. The only way to get back into the game is to double-up. And, since you only get hands of 20 or more points about 25% of the time you must try to make the most of any such hands. In an early position with 20 points or more you should go ahead with the all-bet bet. In a late position this can also work as long as there aren't any big bets ahead of you. If there is a big bet you will want to fold a hand with only 20 or 25 points but go ahead with the all-in bet with higher valued cards.

<u>You have a draw to a winning hand and are low on chips</u>

When your stack is getting low such as between 6 and 10 big blinds the all-in bet may be a good strategy. This would be especially true with hands of 30 to 40 points. These hands are probably only drawing hands but have a lot of potential. You don't want to have a lot of other players to contend with so using the all-in bet is advisable. In most cases you will not be called so you will likely pick up the blinds and any earlier small bets.

Also, when in such a situation and you get even better hole cards on the next hand, another all-in bet will look like a bluff and you are more likely to be called.

<u>You have a sure win hand</u>

A sure win hand is often called the "nuts" but you must be careful about assuming you actually have a sure win before all the community cards are dealt. For instance, when holding a suited Ace and the flop has three of that suits, it would seem that you have the nuts. However, at that point there is still a chance for another player to get a Full House if a card on 4th or 5th street pairs the board. Therefore, in this situation, you would want to make a big bet to drive out other players but you wouldn't want to go all-in yet.

Another situation to be careful with is when you catch a Full House on the flop when your cards are low. For example, assume you are holding:

 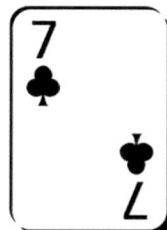

And the flop is:

 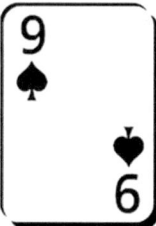 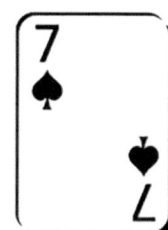

108

You now hold a Full House with 7s over 9s. However, as good as it looks there are a lot of ways to lose this hand. The obvious one is that another player could be holding pocket 9s and therefore have Four-of-a-Kind but this is extremely rare. More common would be another player with a higher pocket pair than your 7s. If you don't drive this player out, he/she could make a higher Full House on 4th or 5th street. A large bet is therefore recommended but I still would not use the all-in bet before all the community cards are dealt.

In fact, there are very few situations where you would truly have the "nuts" after the flop and when that happens you would not want to go all-in right away. Instead, you should make smaller bets to build the pot and wait until after 5th street to use the all-in bet.

<u>You have a pretty good hand and lots of chips and there is only one opponent who is looking weak and has a small stack</u>

There will be situations in which taking a bit of a risk with mediocre hole cards can be justified such as when you have a big stack and have a chance to take out a player with a small stack. You have to be sure there is no opportunity of another player with a large stack to also call the bet.

I have seen this strategy used frequently in the later stages of a tournament. This could be even done with a low pocket pair or a big drawing hand such as A-K.

There are some situations in which you might be tempted to go all-in that should be avoided:

<u>You hold pocket Aces in early position early in the tournament</u>

There is always the temptation to immediately go all-in before the flop when you hold pocket Aces. I have seen a lot of players do this and more often than not all they win are the blinds. Since you only will get pocket Aces every 200 or so hands you need to maximize their potential.

Of course, when in late position and another player has made a big bet, the all-in raise could be utilized before the flop.

There is more on how to play with pocket Aces in chapter 7.

Another player has made a big bet and you only have a draw to a sure win

This is another tempting situation to use the all-in bet. The question is "do you want to risk all your chips on a draw?" Certainly not early in a tournament unless you are already low on chips. It is very hard to give up good cards but hoping to catch cards is not prudent when a lot of your chips might be at stake.

You have caught a set on the flop

When you catch three-of-a-kind on the flop the feeling often is that it must be a sure winner. This will depend a lot on what the other cards are on the flop. Is there a Flush or Straight draw that another player might go for? Would going all-in drive them out? Why risk all of your chips if there is a chance of losing? Instead, you should make smaller bets and see what 4th or 5th street does for you or for any of the other players.

Summary

- The all-in bet must be used very sparingly and almost never as a bluff

- Exception to this rule would be against players with a short stack that you want to eliminate from the tournament

16

Chapter Sixteen

On-line Strategies

When you are playing on-line you don't have the opportunity to look for visible tells by the other players but there are a number of situations that you can take advantage of:

- Player(s) sitting out
- Player(s) on tilt
- Auto-folds

There are also some betting styles to watch for:

- Player(s) who play a lot of hands
- Player(s) who use check-raising a lot
- Player(s) who raise often when on the button
- Player(s) who play very few hands

Players Sitting Out

In on-line games there will be occasions when players are sitting out. This can happen when they get distracted and don't play in the time allotted or they are forced out by being disconnected. Also, there are players who run out of time and have to leave or have lost so many chips they don't care to play anymore.

Regardless of the cause it is a situation you have to watch for and then take advantage of. At some on-line poker sites there is an indication of a player that is sitting out but at others you just have to look for this possibility. One indication of a player sitting out would be continuous quick folds even in situations in which playing is likely such as in the big blind with no raises before the flop. Another would be very quick folds on repeated deals.

Once you have identified a player that is sitting out you can take advantage of this in a number of ways. The most obvious is when that player is in the big blind. If you are in the small blind and all other players have folded before the flop any raise you make will win the hand. In a late position a raise with even poor cards might drive out the players behind you so that you win the blinds. This can be especially helpful when the blinds are fairly large.

Another possibility is when the player sitting out is on the button and you are next to the button. Knowing that this person will be folding allows you to play as though you are on the button and promote your cards accordingly.

Also, when you might be on the cusp of being "in-the-money" playing cautiously might be appropriate in order to let that player "blind-out". Certainly, you would not want to commit a lot of chips unless you have a sure winner.

<u>Player(s) on Tilt</u>

Here is another situation that occurs frequently. Players that experience a "bad beat" will often experience a form or rage which will distort their logic in playing a subsequent hand. This has been referred to as being "on tilt" as people who have played pin ball games know when they shake the machine too much.

A player on tilt will often overplay the next hand or two. One signal that this might be the case would be excessively large bets such as going all-in several hands in a row, especially in an early position. Or it might be several hands in which the players call, or raises, and then losses again with weak cards.

To take advantage of a player on tilt you might call his/her large bet, or even an all-in, with hands that you otherwise would fold, such as a drawing hand like A-Q, a suited Ace, or a small pair.

Or, when in an early position with a strong hand get in with the minimum chips on the expectation that the other player will do something rash.

At the same time, you have to be careful to not get trapped by a cleaver player so you have to try and remember how this player had been acting earlier in the tournament.

<u>Auto-folds</u>

On some of the on-line sites a player can select "fold to any bet", or something like that, well before it is their turn. For instance, if before the flop, and there are no raises around to the player in the big blind and his/her hand checks quickly, it is likely an indication of a weak hand. After the flop when hands are checked very quickly, it is also likely a signal of players that did not get help on the flop.

This can be very helpful in playing your own cards since a bet or raise may well drive out such players. In a late position, with all checks to you, a bet with rags might also win the pot.

<u>Player(s) who play a lot of hands</u>

When you notice that a player is playing a lot of hands it is likely he/she is playing a lot of hands with mediocre holdings. The good news is that you can often win a lot of chips against such a player but you do not want to take excessive risks either. You especially want to watch how this player reacts after the flop and, of course, pay particular attention to how the flop might help someone with mediocre cards.

Where this player is in a short stack position you might call when you don't necessarily have a sure win.

Player(s) who check-raise often

The check-raise bet is generally an indication of a very strong hand however you may run into players who try to overuse this bet to chase people out of hands when they themselves don't have a strong hand. Watching for such players can be helpful so that when you do have a strong hand you can let such a player overplay his/her cards and wait until after 5th street to make a large bet.

Player(s) who raise often when on the button

A player that is on the button is in a powerful position which is why I have given an extra 20 points for this situation. Some players try to take advantage of this by often raising when in this position in order to steal the blinds or by putting themselves in a position to bluff after the flop. When you do have good cards and a player on the button has been raising often, you should check into them.

Or if you are in the big blind with only 20 or so points you normally would fold to a raise before the flop. However, if the player on the button has raised often in that situation, you could call a small raise or even do a re-raise and then adjust your next moves on the assumption the other player has a weak hand.

Even when in other positions, calling a small raise by the person on the button can be justified when holding at least a drawing hand.

Player(s) who play very few hands

As a tournament progresses you will need to be aware of how active the other players have been. When you see that a certain player is getting involved in very few hands you need to be careful when that player does get involved as that is a indication of a strong holding. Before the flop you will need more points to call a bet from such a player. With a large bet you will need 35 to 40 points to call. Even with a small bet you should have more than 20 points to call.

After the flop you must have a very powerful hand to go up against such a player. I would not bet into him/her in an early position at all and let that player show if the flop helped. In a late position you would want to have a strong hand to call any bets by that player.

Summary

- There are a number of tells that don't involve any physical aspects especially when playing on-line

17

Chapter Seventeen

Early Position Strategies

The position at the table has a big impact on your strategy. Some positions need to be handled with a conservative approach while others can be treated aggressively. In the earlier chapters references to such approaches have been made but, in this chapter, we look at this in more detail.

"Under-the-Gun"

The "under-the-gun" position is the player to the left of the big blind. Once the initial two cards are dealt to each player, the person "under-the-gun" is the first to declare their intentions in the hand. At the very least they can "limp-in" by betting an amount equal to the big blind amount. Or, they can bet a larger amount by declaring a raise. (It could even be their whole stack in no-limit games.)

The trouble with this position is the unknown factor of what all the other players might do afterward. When a player who is "under-the-gun" comes into the pot he or she could be raised by any of the following players. The amount of the raise could be significant thus requiring the "under-the-gun" player to decide whether to continue the hand at all. Due to this risk, my system indicates that when in the "under-the-gun" position you need to subtract 10 points from the hand value.

This subtraction forces such a player to have fairly strong cards to get involved. Thus, a player with only 20 basic card points should subtract 10 points and thereby not have enough points to play the hand at all. Similarly, a player with 30 basic card points would have only 20 total points after the subtraction and, as a result, however such a hand is only worth a limp-in approach. Higher valued hands could still warrant a raise in this position.

Most good poker players recognize the inherent risks of playing in the "under-the-gun" position and will therefore play conservatively when they are in that position. And, these players will also assume that an "under-the-gun" player that does come into the hand is likely to have a strong holding.

Of course, there may be times, depending on your situation in the tournament, that you might make a raise in the "under-the-gun" position with mediocre cards as a semi-bluff in the hope of stealing the blinds. When that doesn't happen, you may actually catch something on the flop and be able to continue. In either case a continuation bet after the flop is in order if your raise before the flop was just called. Such a strategy is only recommended later in the tournament after you have already folded a lot of hands when you were under the gun.

"Big Blind"

The big blind position requires that player to put in a designated amount of chips before any cards are dealt. Once all the players receive their two cards, this player is the last to play and therefore gets to see what others players do. When there are no raises, he/she can check and see the flop for free. This can lead to a winning hand even with poor cards if the flop happens to connect well with his/her cards.

When there is a raise before the flop by an earlier player, the person in the big blind must have at least 20 points to call and then only when it is a minimum raise. For larger raises more points are required to stay in the hand.

After the flop this position has the same constraints as the under-the-gun player had before the flop since the big blind player will now be in an early position. If the small blind player had already folded the big blind is the first to play. Being first means, of course, the uncertainty of what the following players might do. With that in mind, this player must have very strong cards to continue.

Another strategy for aggressive players in the big blind is to make a raise before the flop even with only 20 points. This puts them in position to make a continuation bet after the flop to try to drive out the other players.

Summary

- Subtract 10 points when in the "under-the-gun" position
- Big Blind hands are generally first to play after the flop and therefore need a strong hand to continue

18

Chapter Eighteen

Momentum Plays

Even though there are specific odds for a particular card to be the next one dealt, or for you to catch certain cards on the flop, or to win the hand in any given situation, there are also situations where events are repeated. Such as when a craps player gets hot and rolls seven three times in a row. The odds are not very good but it happens. In this chapter we look at a couple of situations in Texas Hold'Em that you might consider in your play.

Repeated Cards

I have noticed that every so often some cards will re-appear for several hands in a row. As an example, let's say a pair of 9s show up on the flop in one hand and then in the next hand another 9 is dealt. On the third hand you catch an unsuited A- 9. Normally this would not be a hand to play but since 9s seem to be hot it might be worth giving it a chance. Certainly not for a lot of chips but with a minimum bet, why not?

Or if you needed a 9 after the flop to fill a straight why not call a small bet to see 4th street?

The same thing can happen with a given suit. When there is a lot of a given suit showing up for a couple hands in a row and you are dealt two of that suit in a subsequent hand, limping-in for a chance at a flush might by justified.

Here is an example of a hand I played where the momentum idea worked. I was in an early position with:

9♥ 6♠   5♣ 5♣

So, I of course folded. Two other players were in the hand when the flop was:

I was disappointed that I hadn't been able to see the flop but as it turned out another player also had a five and won the hand. On the next hand one of the players had:

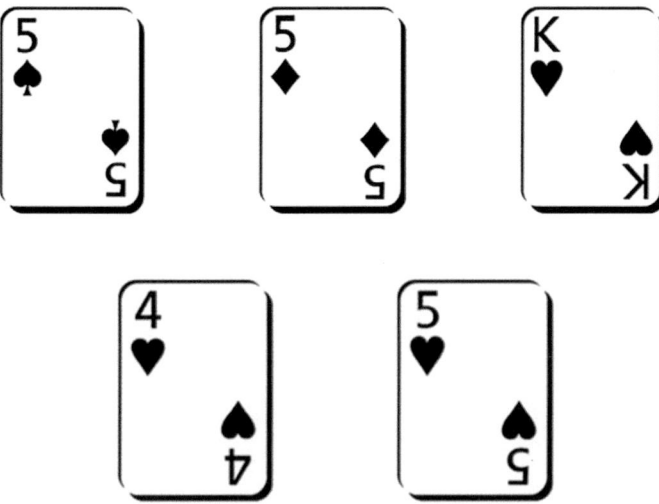

The flop was:

This player went on to win with a full house when a Four showed up on 4th street as well as 5th street. I had noticed that Fives had been frequent so two hands later I was dealt:

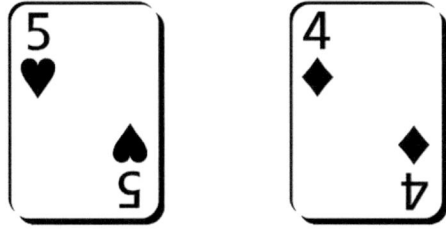

I was in a late position and decided to call a small bet even though such cards were only worth 10 points. There were 4 players in the hand and the flop was:

This turned out to be a very profitable hand.

Winning Streaks

Another possible repeat situation is a winning streak. In a situation where you have won two hands in a row why not get into the next hand with only 10 or 15 points? The players will often shy away if you made a bet after the flop since they might perceive that you are running hot.

In Doyle Brunson's book he says that when he wins a hand, he likes to get involved in the next hand even with marginal cards.

You of course, would not want to risk a lot of chips in these situations but they might generate some winning hands even when you starting cards don't look that good.

At the same time, be aware that other players may get hot as well and play accordingly.

Summary

- Watch for hot cards or hot hands and limp-in whenever possible

19

Chapter Nineteen
To Muck Or Not To Muck

The word "Muck" is a unique term in the world of poker. In Webster's New Collegiate Dictionary, it is defined as manure or that which befouls. For poker it is the discard pile. Thus, when cards are discarded by a player it is referred to as "mucking" the cards.

There are two situations in which a player might choose to "muck" their cards:

- A player has won a hand in which all other players have folded. In this case the winning player does not have to show his/her cards.

- A player has called another player's bet and that player then shows a winning hand. The losing player does not have to show his/her cards and just concedes the pot to the other player.

In both of these situations the hand is finished so that showing one's cards is permitted as compared to when a player folds his/her cards before the hand is finished. As long as there are players still in the hand any player that wishes to quit the hand must only fold his/her cards without showing them.

In the big tournaments some players will show their cards rather than mucking them. Sometimes this is done to show that he/she won the pot with a bluff. Other times, it is done just to let the other player know that they made a good fold. And, thirdly, a player who knows they have lost might show his/her cards to let the other player(s) know that they decided to fold good cards because of the pressure from the betting.

Whatever the situation is it ever wise to show one's cards rather than mucking them?

My opinion is that players should always muck their cards. To show one's cards is to give away information that can harm one's chances of winning a later hand because the other players learned something.

For instance, you make a large bet which causes all the other players to fold. If this bet was a bluff and you show that you were bluffing, the other players will make a mental note of what you had done earlier in the hand. If you had just limped in to see the flop, they get to see what kind of cards you were holding that caused you to just limp in rather than making a larger bet. If your bluff was after 4th or 5th street, they get to see how you played after each subsequent stage of the hand.

Some players think that showing a bluff works to their advantage by putting another player on tilt or that when they might have a good hand in a later deal and make a similar play that the other players might think it is another bluff and call. That, of course, might happen, but I believe the information that is given away outweighs these opportunities.

Another situation in which players might show their cards instead of mucking is when they have won the hand with good cards and are being "friendly" by showing the other player(s) they made a good fold. When I am playing, even is a so-called "friendly" game, I am playing to win and not make friends. Why would you want to make another player feel good about folding? And, as mentioned above, why show the other players how you handled good cards during the different stages of that hand?

For all these reasons I always muck my cards.

Summary

- Cards should always be mucked regardless of the situation

PRACTICE EXERCISES

This chapter provides a few practice exercises in order to help you utilize the strategies described in this book. The answer to each exercise is provided at the end of the chapter.

Exercise 1

You are sitting "under–the-gun" and have been dealt the following hole cards:

Since you are "under-the-gun" you are first to act. What do you do?

a. Fold

b. Limp-in

c. Raise

Exercise 2

You are on the button with the same cards as in exercise 1.

What do you do if there are no raises before your turn?

a. Fold

b. Limp-in

c. Raise

Also, what do you do if there is a raise before your turn?

a. Fold
b. Call
c. Re-raise

Exercise 3

You are on the button with the following cards.

What do you do if there are no raises before your turn?

d. Fold
e. Limp-in
f. Raise

Also, what do you do if there is a raise before your turn?

d. Fold
e. Call
f. Re-raise

Exercise 4

You are in a middle or late position with the following cards:

What do you do if there are no raises before your turn:

a. Fold
b. Limp-in
c. Raise

What do you do if there is a raise before your turn:

a. Fold

b. Call

Exercise 5

You are in a middle or late position with the following cards:

A pocket pair is certainly a hand you don't want to fold so the question is whether to limp-in and hope to catch a set or do you make a raise before the flop?

Or, if there is a raise before your turn, do you just call or make a re-raise?

Exercise 6

You have caught the ultimate hand:

Since such a hand only occurs every two hundred or so times how do you optimize it?

- Make a very large bet right away and hope that another player calls

- Limp-in and try to trap other players

- Make a moderate size raise

Exercise 7:

You are in middle or late position with hole cards of:

These are very low-ranking cards so do you get involved at all?

Exercise 8:

You are in a middle position with:

Do you get involved at all?

Exercise 9:

You limped in with the following cards and two other players also entered:

The flop is:

Another player makes a large bet. What do you do?

a. Fold

b. Call

c. Re-raise

Exercise 10:

Your hole cards are:

You had bet three times the big blind before the flop and were called. The flop is:

The player that called your bet now makes a large raise. What do you do?

a. Fold

b. Call

c. Re-raise

Exercise 11:

You made a raise before the flop with the following cards and were called:

The flop was:

You made a small raise based on your pair of Queens but were then re-raised. What do you do?

a. Fold

b. Call

c. Re-raise

Exercise 12:

You were able to limp in with the following cards:

The flop was:

You now have an Ace-high flush draw. What do you do if another player makes a small bet and what do you do if they make a large bet? Also, if there is no bet ahead of you, what do you do?

Exercise 13:

You are holding the following and have made a raise before the flop which was called by two players:

The flop is:

You now have a very strong hand with a set of tens. You are hoping that one of the other players has caught a pair of Aces or Kings. What should you do:

a. Limp-in

b. Raise

Answers:

Exercise 1:

With an Ace and ten your basic point count is 20 (15 for the Ace and 5 for the ten) but you must subtract 10 points for being under-the-gun. Your net total is therefore only 10 points. In that case your answer is (a) fold the hand. As a reminder, the reason to subtract 10 points when in an early position is the uncertainty of what the following players might do. If, for example, you limped-in with such cards and another player made a raise, what do you do then?

There are a couple exceptions not getting involved in such a hand:

- You have less than five big blinds in your chip stack in which case an all-in bet is recommended.
- Another exception would be when it is the first hand you are playing against the players at this table. In that case a bet of twice the big blind would send a message that you are an aggressive player which could help on subsequent hands.

Exercise 2

The basic value for this hand is 20 points but you must add 20 an additional point for being on the button bringing the total to 40. This qualifies for aggressive play. If there hasn't been a raise when it is your turn, a bet of 3 times the big blind is recommended. If there has been a raise, a re-raise is warranted as long the previous raise was no more than three times the big blind. Otherwise, a call is appropriate.

Exercise 3

Even though this hand has no basic point value, you get to add 20 points for being on the button. Since 20 points is all that is required to get involved in a hand, you can play these types of hands as long as there hasn't been a raise before your turn. So, with no raise, a limp-in bet is appropriate. If neither of the blinds then make a raise you get to see the flop with a minimal commitment.

If there has been a raise before your turn then a fold is appropriate.

Exercise 4

The basic value for this hand is 25 points (15 for the Ace and 10 for the queen). However, 5 points can be added for the small gap thus bringing the total to 30. This qualifies the hand for some aggressiveness. With no raises before your turn a raise of three times the big blind is appropriate.

With a small raise before your turn a re-raise can be ventured. However, when there is a large raise, a call is all that should be undertaken. Keep in mind that even though this hand looks strong it is only a drawing hand so committing a lot of chips before the flop is very risky.

Exercise 5

Any pocket pair of nines or lower is valued at 30 points. This is enough to allow a somewhat aggressive approach. With no raises ahead of you, a bet of three times the big blind is appropriate. You want to drive out most of the other players so you can minimize the number of players to contend with after the flop.

When there is a small raise ahead of you a call is all that should be undertaken since a re-raise would allow the original raiser to fire back with another bet.

With a large raise before your turn a fold would be appropriate since the only way to beat a strong hand is to catch a set on the flop and the odds of that are 1 in 7.

Exercise 6

With pocket Aces, or even Kings or Queens, optimization is important. A big raise before the flop would probably drive out all the other players so that all that is won is the blinds. A limp-in would likely allow several other players to see the flop thus opening the door for someone to catch a better hand such as a straight or even a flush. Instead, the recommendation is to make a raise of three times the big blind. When called, this builds the pot thus allowing you to win more chips if no other player gets lucky on the flop.

Exercise 7:

Suited cards have a value of 10 points and connected cards also have a value of 10 points, so this type of hand is worth 20 points. It is therefore a hand to play but only with a minimal commitment before the flop.

Exercise 8:

Many players seem to think a hand with an Ace is worth playing regardless of the other card. This can lead to a big loss of chips when an Ace shows up on the flop especially and your hole card is a low one. With nine players at a table, eighteen cards of the deck will have been put into play as hole cards. The odds are pretty good than even when you have one of the Aces that another player will also have one, so, with a relatively low kicker you will need additional help to win such a hand. Therefore, I will only get involved with a weak Ace when I am on the button.

Exercise 9:

Even though you now hold two pairs the player making a large bet may well have caught a set of tens. Calling a large bet on the hope of getting a full house would be a high-risk strategy since there are only four cards out of the remaining cards in the deck. The odds of getting one of those cards on 4th street is about 2 to 12. If there was only a small bet ahead of you then calling is a reasonable approach. With a large bet a fold is the best approach.

Exercise 10:

It can be very hard to give up a high pair but, in some circumstances, it is the right thing to do. In this case when a player has made a large bet a fold would be wise. With a small bet by the other player a re-raise would test their strength. You must keep in mind that if the player caught a pair of Aces or kings with the flop you would have to catch one of the two remaining Queens on 4th street or 5th street to win the hand and the odds of that are 1 in 12.

Exercise 11:

Folding a high pair is one of the toughest choices you have to make in Texas Hold'Em. You had 40 points before the flop which justified your raise. But you were called so the other player must have some quality cards. Even with your pair the flop of all of one suit is a big issue. The other player may have caught a flush or be on a draw to a flush. If they make a small bet a re-raise by you will test their strength in case they were bluffing. However, if they make a large raise, a fold would be appropriate.

Exercise 12:

With an Ace-high flush draw you can afford to take some chances especially if there are no large bets ahead of you. A small raise would be in order if there were no bets to call and a call would be appropriate to a small bet. However, when there is a large bet, you have to consider the size of the pot and the odds of filling the flush. There are nine hearts left in the deck if none of the other players had one in their hole cards. Therefore, the odds of catching one of them on 4th street is, at best, about 1 in 5. If you think you could win five times the amount bet, then calling is appropriate.

Exercise 13:

When you catch a set on the flop you need to maximize the hand. Even on the slim chance another player catching a flush or a straight you also have just as good a chance of making a full house. So, in this situation, you should let the other player(s) do the betting and only come in strong after 5th street if there is not straight or flush likely.

20

Chapter Twenty

Quick Thoughts

- Play the first hand in a tournament with any cards if you can limp-in

- After winning a hand play the next hand with only 10 or 15 points

- Be watchful for a possible Full House when a pair is included in the community cards

- Don't bluff a lot when the blinds are small

- Don't bluff when the flop has low cards

- Be careful when another player has a short stack

- Players that bluff often will think other players are bluffing when large bets are made

- Take full advantage of the opportunity to make a re-buy

- When you have a short stack keep track of when the blinds are going up

- When under-the-gun don't just limp-in if you going to play the hand at all. Instead make a raise.

- Don't be afraid to fold big pairs when higher cards are on the board and there are big bets

- Two pairs are not a sure win

- Do not bluff when your stack is only 10 to 20 big blinds

- A suited A-4 is better than an A-7 because of the straight opportunity

- Never show your hole cards if you don't have to

- Don't play when tired. You have to watch every hand and keep track of what the other players are doing so you can utilize that information in subsequent hands

- In a tight table use only small raises with good cards

- When in one of the blind positions be ready to fold when the flop misses you

- Be extra cautions in hands where the flop includes a pair, 2 or 3 of a suit, or 3 to a straight

Glossary

4th Street

- The fourth card dealt into the middle of the table as one of the community cards to be used by all the players. Also referred to as the "turn" card.

5th Street

- The fifth card dealt into the middle of the table as one of the community cards to be used by all the players. Also referred to as the "river" card.

All-In

- Making a bet for all of your remaining chips. Also referred to as "shoving".

Ante

- An amount of chips that all players must put into the pot before the deal. Not always required in some games. When required in tournaments, the amount will increase as play proceeds.

Bad Beat

- A situation in which a player with a very good hand is beaten by another player who completes a better hand with a card on 4th or 5th street.

Big Blind

- The position two places to the left of the dealer.

Bluff

- Making a bet when not holding a good hand.

Burn Card

- A card from the top of the deck that the dealer throws away.

Button

- A marker that indicates who the dealer is.

Call

- To "call" a bet is to put in the same number of chips as bet by a previous player. Also referred to as "calling" a bet.

Community Cards

- The cards in the middle of the table that all players can use to complete their hand.

Connected Cards

- Two cards that are one level apart such as a 9 and an 8.

Continuation Bet

- A bet made by a player similar to his/her previous bet.

Early Position

- The first or second player to the left of the big blind before the flop. After the flop it is the first player after the dealer that is still in the hand.

Flop

- The three cards that are placed face up in the middle of the table for all players to use to make a hand.

Flush

- Five cards of the same suit in no particular order of ranking such as A♥ –J ♥-9♥ -7♥ -6♥. The winning hand where there are two of more flushes is determined by the high card.

Four of a Kind

- Four cards of the same ranking such as 5♠ -5♥ -5♦ -5♣. It is a rare holding but can lose to a higher four of a kind but only if there are two pairs in the community cards.

Full House

- Three cards of the same rank plus two of another rank such as J-J-J and 9-9. This type of hand can only occur when there is a pair in the community cards.

Gap

- Hole cards that are close together but not connected such as a King and a Jack.
- A hand in which only one card is needed to make a straight such as holding an Ace and King when the flop has a Jack and Ten.

Hole Cards

- The two cards that are dealt to each player.

Kicker

- The highest card of a player's hole cards that not otherwise used in making a hand.

Limp In

- A limp in bet is the minimum amount needed to continue playing a hand.

Muck

- The pile of discarded cards. To "muck" one's cards is to throw them away without showing them to any other players.

No Limit

- A type of Hold'Em in which a player can bet all of their chips at any time.

On-The-Button

- The player that is designated as the dealer is commonly referred to as being "On-the-button".

Open-Ended

- A situation in which a player has a hand that includes four cards of a straight and needs another card at either end to complete the straight such as holding a Queen and Jack and the community cards include a Ten and Nine.

Outs

- Cards that are need by a player to make a good hand. The number of outs a player has will dictate how aggressive he/she might want to be in the hand.

Pocket Pair

- When hole cards are of the same level such as two Kings.

Pot Odds

- A computation that compares the odds of winning a hand versus the amount required to call a bet by another player.

Rainbow Flop

- When all three cards of the flop are of different suits.

River Card

- The fifth card that the dealer puts in the middle of the table. Also referred to as "5th street".

Set

- A holding of three (or four) of the same ranking such as J-J-J.

Shove

- To "shove" is to make a bet of all your chips. Also referred to an "all-in" bet.

Small Blind

- The position immediately to the left of the dealer.

Stack

- The pile of chips that a player has available.

Straight

- Five consecutive cards in different suits such as A♣ -2♣ -3♥ -4♠ -5♦. The winning hand is the one with the highest card. In the example including an Ace the high card is the 5.

Straight Flush

- Five consecutive cards in the same suit such as a J-10-9-8-7 of Hearts. This is the best possible type of hand and can only lose to a higher straight flush. When the straight flush is A-K-Q-J-10 it is called a Royal Flush and is the highest hand possible.

Tell

- A mannerism by a player that indicates how strong his/her hand might be.

Three of a Kind

- Three cards of the same ranking such as 7-7-7. It is often referred to as a "set".

Tilt

When a player loses a big pot in an unexpected manner, he/her might go on "tilt" which means that they might act irrationally in subsequent play.

Trap

- A type of strategy in which a player who has a very good hand will make low bets to confuse other players as to the strength of his/her hand in the hopes of later winning a large pot.

Turn Card

- The fourth card placed in the middle of the table by the dealer to be available to all the players still in the hand. Also referred to as "4th street".

Two Pair

- A hand that contains two of one ranking as well as two of another ranking such as 10-10 and 8-8.

Under-The-Gun

- The player immediately to the left of the Big Blind position.

Weak Ace

- Hole cards that include an Ace with the other card being no higher than a Nine.

Appendix

The only pocket card combinations that justify getting involved in a hand:

Card Values	Pair Bonus	Suited Bonus	Connected/Gap Bonus	Total

High Card A

Card Values	Pair Bonus	Suited Bonus	Connected/Gap Bonus	Total
A A	30	30			60
A K suited	25		10	10	45
A K unsuited	25			10	35
A Q suited	25		10	5	40
A Q unsuited	25			5	30
A J suited	20		10		30
A J unsuited	20				20

A 10 suited	20		10		30
A 10 unsuited	20				20
A 9 or lower suited	15		10		25

High Card K

K K	20	30			50
K Q suited	20		10	10	40
K Q unsuited	20			10	30
K J suited	15		10	5	30
K J unsuited	15			5	20
K 10 suited	15		10		25
K 9 or lower suited	10		10		20

High Card Q

Q Q	20	30			50
Q J suited	15		10	10	35
Q J unsuited	15			10	25
Q 10 suited	15		10	5	30

Q 10 unsuited	15			5	20
Q 9 or lower suited	10		10		20

High Card J

J J	10	30			40
J 10 suited	10		10	10	30
J 10 unsuited	10			10	20
J 9 suited	5		10	5	20

High Card 10

10 10	10	30			40
10 9 suited	5		10	10	25
10 8 suited	5		10	5	20

High Card 9 or lower

pair		30			30
suited & connected			10	10	20

Printed by Libri Plureos GmbH in Hamburg, Germany